THE
STRANGER
FROM
MEDINA

WEST ★ TEXAS
SUNRISE

THE
STRANGER
FROM
MEDINA

A Novel

PAUL BAGDON

Fleming H. Revell
A Division of Baker Book House Co
Grand Rapids, Michigan 49516

Published by Fleming H. Revell
a division of Baker Book House Company
P.O. Box 6287, Grand Rapids, MI 49516-6287
www.bakerbooks.com

Printed in the United States of America

Library of Congress Cataloging-in-Publication Data
Bagdon, Paul.
    The stranger from Medina : a novel / Paul Bagdon.
        p.   cm. — (West Texas sunrise ; bk. 3)
    ISBN 0-8007-5835-8
    1. Clergy—Fiction. 2. Sheriffs—Fiction. 3. Texas, West—Fiction. 4.
Ranch life —Fiction. I. Title.
PS3602.A39 S77 2003
813′ .6—dc21   2002152774

This novel is dedicated to a grand group of people who are not only accomplished writers, but treasured friends:

Bonnie Frankenberger	Carole Young
Willow Kirchner	Louise Whitney
Art Maurer	Sid O'Connor
Linda Pepe	Margaret Swann
Emily Altmann	Roz Pullara
Linda Terra	Loren Adams
Joe Callan	Ginny Miller

1

Lee Morgan leaned forward in her saddle, asking for yet more speed from the coal black stallion she was riding at a full gallop. Tears streamed from her eyes—both from fear and from slashing through the oppressive prairie air at the speed of Slick's fastest gait—and were whipped from her face before they reached halfway down her cheeks.

There was another report, this one closer. And then another. The next shot she heard was much louder. Through her tears and the waves of heat rising from the prairie floor, she saw a colored banner. It seemed impossibly far ahead.

She whispered to Slick, the finest horse she had owned in her forty-two years. He was, in fact, the foundation stud horse at her horse-breeding and training operation, the Busted Thumb. Now she feared she was asking Slick for more than he could give.

Her voice transmitted her fear, and in response, the stallion stretched his impossibly long stride even farther. His hooves seemed barely to touch the prairie floor as he coursed over it, his body extended, his head lowered so that it was barely higher than his massive chest. He ran like a greyhound pursuing its prey.

Slick swung sharply to his left without slowing, sliding his body to the side rather than turning it, to avoid a series of prairie dog holes Lee couldn't see in her tear-obscured vision. She barely noticed Slick's maneuver—she merely moved with the animal as if she were a part of him.

Slick's body was covered with sweat, glistening like a polished black diamond. Lee could feel his lungs expand as he drew in great draughts of air, and the rhythm, she realized, was too rapid—she was pushing Slick too hard, for too long.

She applied leg pressure, begging the animal for more speed.

The sight she had seen a half hour ago—the blood, the pallor of the man's face, the tiny throb of pulse like that of a wounded bird—flashed before her. Then the rolling boom of a heavy-gauge rifle reached her ears over the pounding of Slick's hooves. "A little more," she gasped to her horse. "Just a little more, Slick!"

But Slick's gait was less steady. He weaved slightly as he threw himself, sucking air. She felt his pain and cried out to him, thanking him for what he was doing, for his courage, his stamina.

"Just a bit longer, Slick. . . . Just a little bit farther!"

She fervently wished she wasn't wearing the confining, long-hemmed dress she had donned for the celebration. The stiff petticoats under her gave little of the leg contact she was so accustomed to as she rode, and the fabric around her flapped crazily in the wind. *What I wouldn't give for my culottes and a man's work shirt!*

She leaned forward the slightest bit more. "Please, Slick . . ."

2

Marshall Ben Flood held his Sharp's rifle at his right side, the barrel pointing at the ground, the polished cherry-wood stock glinting in the bright July sunlight. He stood casually, but his posture was straight, almost military, and he felt the tension in his body as he squinted at the wooden slab with a black circle painted in its center, 350 yards away.

The noisy music of the festival behind him and the man who stood six feet to his right had faded from his consciousness, as had the acrid stink of burned gunpowder in the hot air. In his peripheral vision, he caught the smooth motion of his opponent raising his rifle, but he didn't move his eyes from the black circle. He could feel the pulsing of a blood vessel at his right temple. He didn't like to lose at anything, and he was a bull's-eye down in the shooting match, with a round yet to be fired.

Monte Krupp, his opponent, was a buffalo hunter—one of the best remaining in the West. He was a small man in a field dominated by giants, a dapper man in a world of crude hunters who shunned bathing and clean clothing. At a lean, wiry 5'4", he was a full eight inches under Ben's height, and he was clean shaven with his hair worn short and well combed, while Ben wore his hair long, the sheen of its blackness threaded with gray. He and Monte had served together in the War Between the States, and the bond between them remained strong.

The group of fifty or so watchers standing twenty feet behind the contestants was as quiet as the inside of an abandoned mine shaft. Coins and folded bills had changed hands surreptitiously before the match had started, and now most of the wagering cowhands and shopkeepers were focused on the target. Out of the corner of his eye, Ben saw one cowboy poke a friend with an unlabelled pint bottle. The second wrangler accepted, checked around to make sure he was unobserved, and took a quick pull of corn liquor. Being caught drinking at a festival put on to raise money to build a church wouldn't do a man's reputation much good with the ladies.

Ben heard a soft, sibilant intake of a breath from Monte, and then the concussion of the rifle report struck him like a hot blast of wind. The strident crash of the discharge softened to thunder as it echoed through the plains on which the town of Burnt Rock rested.

At the target, the town banker, Sam Turner, raised a red flag—meaning a bull's-eye—and dabbed the black ring with white paint where the bullet had struck, then stepped back.

"Nice," Ben commented.

"Not bad," Monte allowed. "Could have been tighter to the middle. Seems like I mighta caught a little breeze on the way."

Ben nodded and crouched, tugging a few strands of grass free from the soil at his feet. He tossed the blades into the air and watched as they drifted cleanly to the earth. Then he raised his rifle. Drawing in a breath, he fixed his sights on the black circle. He began a gentle pressure against the trigger and then felt the slightest bit of coolness on the left side of his face, where a bead of sweat had left a damp trail down his cheek. He eased the barrel of his Sharp's the tiniest bit to the left and fired. The banker raised the red flag and dabbed red paint on the hole in the center of the bull's-eye.

Monte brought his rifle to his shoulder and fired quickly this time, playing the same breeze Ben had counted on. It was a gamble—and a gamble that Monte lost. The breeze had died.

Sam Turner raised the white flag. The score was tied. "All right, fellas," he said. "Let's look at whose bullets struck closest to the center of the bull's-eye."

The men went over to look at the target. "You got it, Ben," Monte said. "That last shot of yours was dead center." He held out his hand. "Nice shooting."

"I got lucky. Air touched me as I was squeezin' off that round. You did some great shooting, Monte."

The buffalo hunter turned to the crowd and pointed toward Ben. Applause broke out, along with some cheering and some groans. No one needed the banker to haul the target back for official measurement—the eyes of the two shooters were all anyone needed for verification as to who won the contest.

"I'll tell you what," Monte said with a grin. "If you buy me a glass of lemonade and a piece of Missy Joplin's carrot cake, I won't hold a grudge about today's match."

Ben returned the smile. "You got a deal, Monte. Let's—"

Three quick shots stopped his sentence. Ten seconds passed, and then three more shots sounded. Ben was already in motion, running to where he'd tied his horse, Snorty, in the shade of a few trees near the bandstand.

A black horse, stretched and running hard, pounded toward the festival site, a finger of brown dust trailing behind. The rider was sliding a carbine back into the saddle scabbard.

"Ain't that Miss Lee?" a cowhand shouted. "She's really burnin' up the ground with ol' Slick—it must be somethin' powerful important!"

Lee was leaning forward in her saddle. Ben threw Snorty into a gallop toward her, the muscular legs of the tall horse taking large bites out of the distance between them. Almost as if they'd choreographed it, their horses slid to a stop, placing Lee and Ben side by side.

"Where's Doc?" Lee shouted, her voice cracking with emotion. "Rev Tucker is hurt bad—shot several times. He's bleeding terribly! He . . ." A rush of tears choked her voice.

Ben put his hand on her arm. "Where is he?"

She swallowed hard and drew a breath. "About halfway to the Thumb. I couldn't lift him onto Slick, and I was afraid to move him, anyway. He's gutshot, Ben, and he's bleeding real bad!"

Ben looked back at the festival. "There's Doc's surrey, so he's here. Find him and send him out. I'll go on ahead and see what I can do for Rev."

"I . . . I couldn't lift him, Ben. He's such a big man. His horse was gone, and I . . ."

"You did the right thing. Now go, Lee—find Doc!"

Ben wheeled Snorty around, pointed him in the direction from which Lee had come, and banged his spurless heels against the animal's sides. Snorty wasn't the type of horse that needed spurring; he was in a full gallop within ten yards.

Lee dragged a sleeve across her face and cued her horse toward the crowd. Dripping sweat and drawing air in huge, raspy gulps, Slick didn't question her command.

"Doc!" Lee hollered as she approached the crowd. "Doc!"

The blistering sun beat on Ben and his horse like a club, drawing sweat from every pore. He reined back from the gallop, knowing that even Snorty couldn't take that killing pace on the open prairie.

Far ahead, he saw dark spots scribing circles high in the air. In spite of the heat, he shivered. When two of the spots separated from the others and swept downward, he lengthened his mount's stride.

The two buzzards on the ground hadn't yet desecrated the body of the circuit-riding pastor. The birds lumbered away as Ben approached, their six-foot-long wings struggling to pull their hunched, misshapen bodies into the air.

Ben crouched next to Reverend Tucker. The man's body, a half dozen inches over six feet tall and weighing over three hundred pounds, seemed to have shrunk in death, as if the departure of his life and spirit had diminished his physical stature. Ben touched the pastor's neck artery to check for a pulse, but he did it as a matter of course. He'd seen enough bodies to recognize the presence of death. Gently, he closed his friend's eyes and knelt in the sand beside him. Snorty, ground tied a few feet away, pushed his muzzle at a patch of desiccated buffalo grass as Ben prayed.

Not many words passed between Lee and Doc as they jolted and jerked over the prairie in the battered surrey. Doc wasn't much of a talker, and Lee was alone in her mind. Images of the wounded pastor swirled in her head, and she clenched her hands on the fabric of her dress.

It had been a while since she'd wondered if she'd done the right thing—the prudent thing—in leaving Virginia and moving her horse operation to Texas. Raised by Noah Morgan, the great-grandson of Justin Morgan, she knew horses as well as any man. Uncle Noah had devoted his life to improving the Morgan horse breed, and Lee had worked at his side.

She'd loved Uncle Noah and his family dearly. Still, the inevitable clashes about the direction of his ranch had hurt them both. Lee's dream to breed strong, intelligent horses for ranch work and Uncle Noah's devotion to the Morgan breed had led to differences that couldn't be reconciled. But that didn't diminish the love and respect between them or the gratitude Lee felt toward her uncle for taking her in after her parents were killed.

Lee had known that she'd have to move West to pursue her dream. And she'd known that the West was untamed. She'd read about the range wars, the gunfighters, the bands of bloodthirsty people who preyed on settlers. She'd spent hours talking with Uncle Noah's friends who'd spent time in Texas. She'd prayed for guidance.

And when she'd made her decision, there was a finality to it that was intimidating—almost frightening—but it also reinforced her own feelings about herself and her life. Her gender hadn't held her back in her work with Uncle Noah, and she wouldn't allow it to do so anywhere else.

Still, the violence she'd seen since moving to Texas appalled her. The guns that rode on the hips of many of the people she encountered, the quick, mindless confrontations that often ended with a man bleeding into the prairie or the streets of Burnt Rock, were things she could not get used to.

Why Reverend Tucker? Why would anyone kill a man of God? Were there simply too many guns, too many men who had no more respect for life than a rattlesnake? Was the ground so stained with blood that—

"Lee? Is that the butte you were talking about?"

Doc's voice sounded far away. Pain shot up her arms as she released her clenched fists. "Just beyond it," she said.

When they rolled to a stop near Reverend Tucker's body, Ben was fifty yards away, checking hoofprints and picking up spent shell casings. He looked down at the brass in his palm and then threw the shells out into the prairie.

Lee ran to meet him and stepped into his embrace. She burst into tears. "I don't understand this!" she sobbed. "He was such a good man."

Ben didn't say a word. He just held her close until her sobs subsided. Then he led her over to Doc.

Doc stood over Reverend Tucker's corpse, his eyes squinting against the sun as Lee and Ben approached.

15

"Rev's been dead a couple of hours," he said. "Lee, could you give me a minute with Ben?"

"He was almost gone when I found him," Lee said. "I hoped that if I got you out here, Doc, maybe there'd be a chance . . ." She sniffled the last of her tears and wiped her face with her sleeve. "I'm not a fading flower," she said in answer to his question. "Please say what you need to say."

Doc held her steady gaze for a moment, then nodded. "There are three broken arrows in Rev, but the majority of the damage was done to him by bullets." He shifted his eyes to Ben. "Does that tell you anything?"

"Yeah. It does. There are lots of tracks out here, and about half of them were made by unshod horses, probably Indian ponies. I found some shell casings too. They were mostly 30.30 Confederate army issue."

"Rebs? How can you tell?" Doc asked.

Ben took a cartridge case from the pocket of his vest and tossed it to Doc. It glinted in the sun in its short arc between the two men. "Toward the end of the war the Rebs were runnin' real short on metals and were producin' shells that were almost all brass 'cause they couldn't get the base metals they needed. That's why these are so shiny."

"But the war's been over a dozen years," Lee said.

"That's my point. Just before Appomattox, hundreds of Rebs just walked away from the army, and they took guns and ammo with them. Most went home and tried to put their lives together. Some didn't—they stashed what they'd stolen and gathered into groups like the Night Riders and just kept right on killin'."

"You figure that's who did this?" Doc asked.

"I'm sure of it. The army shells and the arrows bear it out too. Some renegade Indians joined up with some night riders."

Lee felt her fingers clenching her dress again. "Is the town in danger?"

"I doubt it," Ben answered. "If this band was gonna raid Burnt Rock, they wouldn't have announced themselves by killing Rev."

"Then why did they kill him?"

Ben shook his head. "'Cause he was there, I guess. Ridin' that big ol' gelding of his and probably singin' a hymn at the top of his lungs like he always did . . ." He turned away for a moment, gazing out into the distance. When he faced Doc and Lee again, his face was hard. "Let's get Rev on the wagon an' get back to town. I want to put a few men out on guard just to make sure this bunch ain't gonna surprise us tonight."

"Are you going after them then?" Lee asked.

"First light tomorrow. I figure there were maybe six or eight of them, and their tracks show they were ridin' hard away from here. I'll hang tight tonight and see what I can find tomorrow. I need to wire to the jurisdictions around us and the army too, to let them know we've been hit here."

It hadn't taken the citizens of Burnt Rock long to clean up the festival site. When Ben rode past it an hour and a half later on his way into town, the banner reading "Church Fund Festival" looked forlorn in spite of its cheerful colors. The tables that had held the pies, cakes, and pastries were gone, quickly loaded onto farm wagons and taken into town, leaving behind only the indentations of their legs in the sand. A burlap sack nestled at the base of one of the poles holding the banner, apparently missed by the cleanup crew. Bits of straw skittered about in the slight breeze. The fun and laughter and excitement that had been there only a few hours ago had died along with Rev Tucker.

Ben rode slowly toward the end of Main Street and the partially framed skeleton of the church. Most of the folks who'd been at the celebration had gathered there, perhaps feeling the comfort a church—even an incomplete one—offers in times of death. Ben sat on Snorty to address the crowd.

"It was marauders—night riders—who killed Rev Tucker," he said. "I'm gonna ask some of you men to stand guard with me around town tonight, but I'm not expectin' more trouble. Bands like these are cowards and scavengers who do more fightin' with each other than they do with anyone else. They pick off travelers and peddlers, and maybe a stagecoach every so often, but they're not nearly brave enough to take on a town. I'll be ridin' around town tonight, and I'll go after them tomorrow."

"You gonna mount a posse, Marshall?" a man asked.

"No need," Ben answered. "Ain't but six or so of 'em. Just sit tight and try to go on like you usually do. That's all I can say for now."

Ben turned Snorty around. The crowd began to break up as he headed toward his office. As he rode at a walk past the depot, he noticed there was a loaded lumber car on the siding. That was good; work on the church had slowed in the past week due to lack of boards and beams. Lumber was hard to come by this far west, but the new link and depot built in Burnt Rock by the Trans-Texas Rail Road offered access to faraway markets.

Ben knew that the TTRR was a boon to the ranchers and farmers around Burnt Rock as well. Cattle drives were expensive and cut deeply into the money a rancher needed to keep his operation going. The farther a herd walked and the longer they sweated under the sun, the less they weighed at shipping time. Benton, the next town from which herds could be loaded onto cattle cars, was better than two hundred miles beyond Burnt Rock, and much of the way was hard traveling. Because the two-hundred-mile trek could be cut from the journey to market, Burnt Rock was becoming a bustling cow town. Farmers, too, benefited from the railroad, since the TTRR was linked to a multitude of other relatively small lines. Farm families could now deliver their grain and produce to hungry markets in the larger cities of Texas.

Louisiana lumber from the thousands of acres of pine forests could now reach Burnt Rock by rail at a better price than if it were shipped from within Texas. The aromatic scent of the cut wood reached Ben, and he breathed it deeply. It was a fine, fresh smell, but for the smallest bit of a moment, it evoked the memory of trees being cut at Bull Run for cover just before the battle. He shook the memory away.

Snorty attempted to swing over to the watering trough in front of the Drovers' Inn, but Ben held him back and directed him down the street. Most of the businesses along Main Street had closed for the festival and remained closed after Rev's death was announced. O'Keefe's Café, Scott's Mercantile, the Burnt Rock Land and Trust Company, Clara's Dresses for Madam, and the restaurant attached to the Merchant's Rest Hotel were locked and lightless. But even at the dinner hour, the Drovers' Inn was doing good business: drunken laughter rolled out to the street past the batwing doors, and the acrid scent of tobacco smoke, alcohol, and sweat enveloped Ben like a cloud of swamp gas.

Ben turned down the alley by his office and the three-celled jail to the fenced lot where Snorty spent his spare time. There, Ben drew a half bucket of fresh water for his horse and stripped off his tack while he drank. Ben roughed Snorty's coat with a grain sack, allowing the breeze to reach his flesh, and the horse grunted like a sow in a mud bath.

Ben entered his office through the back door and walked past the empty cells and into the front room. His desk was awash in WANTED posters. He sat in the chair, and the wood creaked under him, as it always did. On his desk a mug of coffee he'd abandoned hours ago rested on the editorial page of the *Burnt Rock Express*. He hefted the mug and drained it, savoring the harsh, outdoorsy flavor of the coffee. Heat, in his mind, was no more important to coffee than wrappings were to a gift. He picked up a pencil and began composing his wire to Fort Kaiser, the nearest army encampment, and to the other towns around Burnt Rock, on the back of a wanted poster.

When he was just about finished, Lee pushed open the office door from the street and stood framed in the doorway. As always when he saw her, he drew in a sharp breath. The dark luster of her long hair, the piercing intensity and warmth of her deep chestnut eyes, and the permanently tanned features of her high-cheekboned face never ceased to stun him.

She crossed the office and sat in the chair next to his desk. There were trails through the grit on her face down her cheeks. Without speaking, she extended her right hand to Ben, and he took it, cradling it gently in his own.

Lee spoke, her voice husky with emotion. "Remember when Rev slept at old Laphraim Miller's place and then preached the next morning at the Gordons' house?"

Even though tears glittered in her eyes, the beginnings of a smile toyed with the edges of her mouth. "That's what popped into my mind as I walked here from the livery stable."

Ben smiled. "Sure—an' Lap didn't mention that his three hounds slept on the bunk Rev used that night. Rev was teachin' from Romans and was squirmin' and itchin' and scratchin' so's it was impossible to follow what he was sayin'! Was the kids who started laughing first, but then we all . . ."

Lee nodded. "Then Rev started with that big, booming laugh of his and promised never to sleep at Lap's again and started in on how Lucifer's legions are like waves and plagues of fleas, and how . . ."

Her voice trailed off. There was a comfortable silence between them for a long moment.

"Things are gonna be different without him," Ben finally said.

"Yes. They are." Lee paused. "But as horrible as losing Rev is, we can't let it stop progress on the church. He wouldn't want that to happen."

"We won't. But I think we need to realize that we've got to have a full-time man of God in Burnt Rock. When I talked with Rev last week, he said that he felt his real mission was to travel the circuit as he'd been doing for years, not to settle into a town with a single congregation."

"His heart was too big to serve only a handful," Lee agreed. "It was really only because we needed him so badly that he agreed to give us a week or so a month."

"Right. And the way Burnt Rock's growing, even the time Rev could give us wouldn't have been enough."

Lee straightened in her chair. "I'll start writing to theological schools tomorrow. And I'll pay whoever we find the first year's salary too. I've had two good years at the

Busted Thumb, and the army just put in a purchase order for seventy head of remount stock. I've felt kind of . . . I don't know . . . homeless since our little church burned down. It wasn't much, but it was a place we could meet and pray and hold services. Now that I've made some profit, I want to get our church going again, stronger than ever."

Ben squeezed her hand. "That's great, Lee. It shouldn't be too awful long before the church building is finished. Willy Teller said he'd give us the use of his grandpa's little house for Rev or any other minister we got here, so we've got a good situation to offer a man of God."

The office door slammed open and crashed against the wall. Ben was on his feet, and his Colt had cleared leather by the time the door bounced back.

Old Missy Joplin pinned her stare on him. "You might use that weapon on the scoundrels who murdered Rev Tucker rather than on an innocent and defenseless old lady, Benjamin."

Ben holstered his pistol and sat back down behind his desk as Lee stood to embrace the old woman.

"You're about as innocent and defenseless as a mama bear, Missy," Ben said. "And I've asked you a dozen times not to come chargin' in here like a bull buffalo! You like to give us both heart attacks!"

"Oh, hush," Missy said, dismissing him with a wave of her hand and moving into Lee's hug. "I'm so sorry it was you who had to find Rev, honey. What a terrible thing for you."

Missy Joplin stood barely five feet tall; she was as lean and as hard as a railroad spike, and her hair was a constant snowy battle of tangles and wisps. Her skin was gnarled like the shell of a walnut, and her eyes were an unwavering aqua blue that would have been devastating to men on a woman three-fourths her age. As it was, at ninety years old, Missy had more energy and gumption than any other woman of any age in Burnt Rock.

Missy released Lee and turned to Ben, removing a paper sack from her purse. "This is the money from the festival," she said. "There's almost eight hundred dollars—and that'll buy a lot of boards and nails and such."

"Eight hundred dollars?" Lee gasped. "That can't be right! Selling a few cakes and pies doesn't—"

"How much did you toss in on top of the festival money, Missy?" Ben asked, grinning.

"That's none of your business, Benjamin. You just get the order out for what we need—and do it today."

"Yes'm," Ben replied, feeling like a schoolboy answering his teacher.

Lee grabbed onto Missy's hand, acting more like an excited schoolchild. "I'm going to write to divinity schools," she said. "We need to get a minister here as soon as we can."

"Good. An' don't you dare settle on some ol' fogey like me! We need a devoted young fella to boot the fear of the Lord into some of these Sunday Christians hereabouts!" She shook Lee's hand. "I don't expect you need a ride in my surrey back to the Busted Thumb?"

"No, but thank you anyway. I have Slick down at the livery stable."

Missy snorted. "I'm sure you have—and I'm sure you know how I feel 'bout a Christian lady ridin' astride a horse like a common cowhand. And those sinful trousers you insist on wearin' don't do nothin' but give men the wrong idea about you, Lee Morgan."

Lee sighed. "They're *culottes,* and they're not sinful," she said. "I'm more covered than I'd be if I were wearing a dress. In France the women all wear—"

"We're not in France," Missy interrupted. "I understand that the French eat horse meat. Are you going to start doing that too?"

"Missy . . ."

The old lady turned to the doorway. "You see that those letters go out to find that preacher, Lee," she ordered. "And Ben, are you going out after them who murdered Rev Tucker?"

"First thing in the morning."

"You'd be well advised to carry your Sharp's and not try to engage those animals at handgun range, Benjamin. I'll pray for you tonight."

Before Ben could respond, the woman was out the door, her heels tapping hurriedly on the wooden sidewalk as she hustled to her next stop.

"I guess we've been told," he said.

Lee smiled. "Just like always." She turned to the door. "I should head back to the Thumb. I need to tell Carlos and Maria and my men about Rev."

Ben moved to her and drew her gently to him. "I'll stop the day after tomorrow or maybe the day after that."

Lee stepped back from his embrace. "Be careful, Ben."

"I will—you know that. Now that you're in my life, I'm always careful."

As she rode back to her ranch through the twilight, Lee dreaded telling Carlos and Maria, her ranch manager and his wife, about the death of the circuit-riding minister. Rev had spent many nights at Carlos and Maria's home adjacent to Lee's on the Busted Thumb Horse Farm.

Slick moved easily under Lee in his rocking-horse lope. The thud of the stallion's hooves on the arid surface of the prairie sounded like the somber, measured beat of a funeral drum. The sky to the west was ablaze with the setting sun, and she watched the brilliance of the colors as the light diminished. For a moment, her heart was lifted beyond her sorrow and her fear for Ben that she locked away in a secret part of her heart.

But the thoughts returned. *Could I bear that fear for the rest of my life? Could I live with knowing my husband faced death at the hands of evil men every day—and knowing that his work often forced him to kill?* Lee shook her head sharply in an attempt to chase her concerns from her mind. The images and the fears persisted for a moment, but she broke free of them when she straightened in her saddle and cued Slick to run. *That's the only kind of running I do,* she assured herself. *And it's the only kind I will ever do.*

She focused her eyes and her spirit on the sunset and rode on toward her home.

The next morning Snorty was asleep, standing at the corner of his stall, when Ben walked into the small barn with a lantern swinging from his hand. He poured a ration of crimped oats with molasses into his horse's grain pan and checked the level of water in the bucket hanging from its handle in the stall. He separated a flake of hay from a bale, sniffed it to be sure there was no dust or rot, and then dropped it into the stall.

The rich aroma of the horse feed and the strong, warm scent of well-cared-for leather were smells Ben knew he would never tire of experiencing. He sipped coffee from the steaming mug in his hand and watched Snorty eat for a few moments. Then he sat on the dirt floor under the spot where he'd hung his lantern and took a worn, well-thumbed Bible from a shelf where it rested beside a pound can of petroleum hoof dressing and a couple of hoof picks.

It was his system—or nonsystem—to open his Bible to a random page each morning and begin his reading at that spot. Actual Scripture study he left for the meetings he and Lee had begun at her ranch and that now were held at Grange Hall. His morning readings were a pure and necessary pleasure, like a dipper of frigid well water after a long ride across the Texas prairie in mid-August. He breathed a quick prayer of gratitude as he opened the book. There had been no trouble from the raiders or anyone else the night before.

When he closed the Bible and stood, his mind was free—at least for a little while—of his concerns and fears and sorrow over the loss of his friend. He saddled and bridled Snorty and led him outside, where the pastels of dawn were hardening into the brighter, more vibrant colors that preceded the sun. The morning air was cool, but Ben knew the temperature would start climbing in a couple of hours.

Burnt Rock was just rubbing the sleep from its eyes as he rode out of town. At a slow lope he covered the miles to the site where Rev Tucker had been killed, saving Snorty's strength, not knowing how much ground he'd need to cover before nightfall.

The hoofprints in the sand were distinctive enough. Again, his eyes picked out the imperfect oval imprints of unshod horses and the more crisp, inverted Us of the shod animals. Ben put Snorty into a lope and followed the prints as easily as he'd follow a marked road.

Small clusters of clear glass glittering in the strengthening sun indicated that the gang of murderers was drinking whiskey and using the empty pints for target practice. The mindless arrogance of the gang set Ben's mouth in a grim line. They'd murdered a man of God, stolen his horse, and were now meandering to their next bloodletting, making no attempt to cover their tracks.

Ben reined in, dismounted, and hunkered down, using his forefinger to test the tracks. The impressions were still clean—the dirt hadn't yet sifted in to fill them. He couldn't tell how far behind he was, but the spacing of the tracks showed the killers were moving more slowly.

At about noon, he stopped and climbed down from his saddle. He loosened the girths and checked under the saddle blanket for galls, at the same time allowing fresh air to reach Snorty's back. Then he filled his Stetson with water and held it steady as his horse drank from it. Ben took a pair of swallows from the canteen, replaced the cork, and tied it back on his saddle. He wanted more water, but he swallowed his thirst; he wasn't sure when he'd strike water, so rationing was necessary.

During the midafternoon, he noticed what he thought was an injured bird flapping its white wings on the prairie floor a few hundred yards ahead. He eased Snorty into a gallop, thinking he could put the bird out of its pain. When he drew closer, he saw that it wasn't a bird at all—it was a Bible that had been tossed aside. It rested on its back, open wide, and a ground breeze was now ruffling the pages. He dismounted and picked up the book. The inscription inside the front cover read:

To my beloved son, the Reverend
Morris Tucker, who now carries
the truth with him,
just as this book does.

Mrs. Bernard Tucker
June 12, 1851

27

Ben put the remains of the Bible in his saddlebag. When he swung into his saddle, a vein at his right temple began throbbing in tempo with his pulse. That evening he paid scant attention to the splendor of the sunset that engulfed the western sky. His eyes swept the vastness of the prairie around him, never still, seeking out any sign of the gang. He no longer watched for tracks; the murderers had ridden dead west since they'd left Rev's body, and Ben doubted they'd switch directions. After darkness fell, he came upon a small, shallow spring and let Snorty drink. Then he filled his canteen with the tepid, muddy-tasting water and rode on.

The moon, so large and so close in the sky that it seemed he could reach out and touch the stark white fullness of it, provided all the light he needed. A couple of hours past midnight, he heard the distant echo of gunfire—two single rounds and then a volley of pistol and rifle reports. Ben cued Snorty out of his mile-eating lope and into a gallop. The horse responded with a burst of speed and power that carried him over the prairie like a mountain cat following the strong scent of prey.

A few more shots helped Ben center in on precisely where the raiders were located. He topped a small rise, and a wisp of smoke reached him a moment before he saw the fire. It was a large one, with flames reaching well into the sky, the smoke thick and gray in the moonlight. The night riders were burning a farm wagon and whatever it had been carrying. There'd been no ruts as Ben tracked the gang, so the wagon must have been coming from the opposite direction.

Ben drew rein and ground tied Snorty. He didn't loosen the girths this time—he had no way of judging how fast he'd need to get away from the battle he knew was about to take place. He checked the load in his Colt and dropped it back into the holster. Then he slid his Sharp's from its saddle scabbard and pocketed a handful of the large, dome-tipped bullets that weighed nearly an ounce apiece.

There was a rise to the left of the bonfire, perhaps seventy-five yards from the gang's camp. Ben walked to it, his eyes focused on the fire and the figures that were silhouetted around it. A man lurched, stumbled, and fell into the flames, launching a cloud of embers and ash into the sky. He screamed, his voice louder than the raucous laughter and hoots of his outlaw partners. Ben watched as the man scrambled out of the conflagration, shirt ablaze, and dropped to the dirt, rolling, flailing his arms and legs and screaming like a tortured animal.

Ben stretched out on the night-cool dirt on the lip of the rise and jacked a round into the chamber of his buffalo rifle. He placed his Colt carefully beside him, resting the pistol on a patch of dried grass.

His first round tore into the base of the bonfire, pitching into the air burning embers, large chunks of wood, and bits and shards of glass that served Ben as effectively as a load of canister from a cannon. Whatever the wagon owner had been hauling, it was contained in bottles. Ben put another shot into the flames while the shrapnel from his first round was still in the air. Curses melded with the thunderous boom of the Sharp's and the rolling echo it created.

"Throw your weapons out toward me and put up your hands! You're under arrest!" Ben bellowed. A volley of pistol and rifle fire answered; geysers of sand and grit erupted from the ground around and in front of him, and bullets buzzed past his prone form like angry hornets. He fired at a muzzle flash and heard the deep *thunk* of a bullet striking flesh. He focused his next rounds on the point where most of the muzzle flashes were coming from, moving the lever of the Sharp's quickly but without haste, directing the massive slugs calmly, almost mechanically.

"Stop shooting!" a hoarse voice yelled from the camp. "Stop shooting! You're gonna kill us like dogs! We give up!"

"Throw your guns out and walk toward me with your hands up!"

A rifle and two pistols flew out a few yards from the fire and dug into the sandy soil. Three men with their hands up stumbled toward Ben. He reloaded the Sharp's as the killers approached him and then stood, his Colt back in its holster and his rifle tucked into his shoulder, ready to fire.

The shots Ben had anticipated came from the right of the fire, away from the light it gave. He knew those snakes would send at least one man into the dark to ambush him after he'd moved in. The flashes gave him perfect targets. He fired once and then again. Now the only sounds were those of the crackling fire.

"Where's the man who was driving the wagon?" Ben demanded.

"At the bottom of the fire," one outlaw snarled. "In hell."

The muzzle of the Sharp's swung to the man's chest, and for a moment Ben's trigger finger began to exert pressure. He spat to his side as if clearing his mouth of a foul taste as he eased his finger out of the trigger guard.

It was up to the State of Texas to hang these killers. His job was simply to bring them in.

3

Lee drove the big buckboard through the buffalo grass of the prairie, pretending not to notice when one or the other of the two fat old geldings that pulled her reached down to the side and snatched a mouthful of the dewy, knee-high grass. She grinned; it looked so fresh and tender she could almost taste it herself.

It'd been a prosperous summer so far for the Busted Thumb. Her men were sure of a second—and possibly even a third—cutting of hay, and her horses were fat and sleek and healthy.

She adjusted her Stetson so that it shaded her eyes a bit more and reread the list she'd taken from the pocket of her chambray work shirt. The monthly trek to Scott's Mercantile for provisions was generally something she delegated, but the ranch had been running so flawlessly that she welcomed the trip to Burnt Rock.

She glanced down at the cloth bag with a silver clasp that rode on the plank seat next to her. It contained four more letters in her own hand that she'd written the night before at her kitchen table, under the light of a kerosene lamp. Each was addressed to administrators of different schools of theology, and each set forth in detail what the community of Burnt Rock could offer a resident preacher. Seventeen previous letters had gone out in the past couple of months. An equal number of "thank you for your interest, but . . ." return posts were filed in Lee's small office.

Lee chided herself for worrying. She sat a bit straighter and nudged the geldings to pick up their pace. "Come on, you two," she told the horses. "It'll be Christmas before we—"

That's when she saw the boy.

He'd topped a rise, and for a moment, before he started down, he stopped and dragged a sleeve across his forehead. He was fifty yards from the buckboard, and even at that distance Lee could see he was dressed in clothes that hadn't been purchased for him. The sleeves of the stained work shirt he wore were rolled up several times but still reached to the middle of his hands. His denim pants could have accommodated two people his size and were held up by a knotted piece of baling twine. His hat, its too-narrow brim offering little shade to his face, was a bowler of some sort and rested atop his ears.

Lee instinctively reached toward the rifle at her feet and then hissed at herself. Instead, she raised the hand that had started toward the weapon in a wave. The boy hesitated and then waved back. Lee reined her horses toward him and stopped the wagon a few feet away.

The boy's hair was black, long, and greasy, but turned almost gray by the dust that permeated it. His skin had a copper cast to it. He was thin but not gaunt, about Lee's height. His eyes were black and seemed to move constantly, settling on Lee's open gaze for the shortest of moments. It was impossible for her to predict his age; he could have been twelve or seventeen or anywhere in between.

"Going to Burnt Rock?" she asked.

His voice sounded older than he looked. "That's the next town, ain't it, ma'am?"

Lee nodded.

"That's where I'm goin', then," he said. "How far is she?"

"Another three miles or so due west." For some reason the boy made her nervous. *Maybe it's the man's voice in the boy's body,* she thought. "Not far," she added, simply to have something else to say. She knew the protocol of the West as well as the boy did: You didn't leave a person on foot in midsummer on the prairie if you were going in the same direction he was. "Can you drive?" she asked.

"Sure," the boy said with a grin. Lee noticed his teeth were bad—angled in his mouth, yellowed, and with a front incisor missing. He dropped the smile quickly, as if he knew Lee was inspecting his teeth.

"I'm Lee Morgan. What's your name?"

"Henry."

"Just Henry?"

"I got no folks, Miss Morgan. Henry's all I go by."

Lee shifted over on the seat and pulled the rifle in front of her with her foot. "C'mon, Henry," she said, holding the reins toward him, "let's go to Burnt Rock."

The boy hesitated again, as he had before he waved, but then he climbed on to the buckboard. He took the reins, clucked to the geldings, and set out. A silence rose between them, but it wasn't uncomfortable. When they'd gone a mile, Henry took a wrap on the reins with his left hand and dug out a small sack of tobacco and rolling papers with his right.

"I don't hold with smoking, Henry," Lee said.

The boy nodded and continued building a cigarette. His hands were quick and practiced. In a moment he had the cigarette in his mouth, and he scratched a lucifer to light it. Lee shifted to look more directly at him. "I told you I don't hold with smoking," she repeated.

Henry met her eyes for a moment before his glance flicked away. "Lots of folks don't. Don't mean I agree with 'em. You don't wanna smoke, Miss Morgan, that's up to you."

"That cigarette is going to cost you some hot walking in the sun unless you put it out," Lee said.

Henry reined in and handed the lines to her. He stepped down from the buckboard and blew a perfect smoke ring in the still air. "You watch yourself, Miss Morgan. Thanks for the ride," he said.

Lee flapped the reins lightly on the backs of the horses. "You'd best watch yourself too, Henry."

She could feel his eyes on her back as she drove off.

"He was the strangest kid, Ben. So I left him there with his cigarette. Then when I got to town, Mr. Scott told me a couple of his men had gone fishing and that he was short of help. It'll be at least a couple of hours until my buckboard is loaded."

Ben laughed. "If those are the worst problems you ever have, you're in real good shape," he said. "Anyway,

I'm glad you're here. Isn't often I get to ride my rounds with a pretty lady next to me. 'Course, it cost me a good piece of money to get you suitably mounted. That ol' horse OK? Think you can handle him?"

Lee laughed delightedly. "How the livery gets twenty-five cents for a couple hours of this poor old fellow's time is beyond me—and no, I can't handle him. I'm scared he'll run off with me." She reached ahead and affectionately patted the aged chestnut's neck. "You'll be old and tired one day, Ben Flood," she said.

"Already am."

She stood in her stirrups. "Looks like there's a lot going on at the church. Let's see who's doing what. Isn't that John?"

"'Stumbles,' you mean?"

"Ben! You stop that! He can't help that he's a little clumsy. He's a great teacher, and he loves the kids."

John Stiles grunted under the weight of the rough-hewn beam he carried as he backed carefully across the elevated stage upon which the choir of the new church would one day perform. Billy Strummer, a burly crew chief for the Trans-Texas Rail Road, carried the other end of the twelve-foot beam. On the far side of the church, a group of six men muscled a framed, ten-foot section of wall upright from where it had been con-structed on the ground, sliding it on the base plate of the foundation of the skeletal building. The section seemed to be growing heavier rather than lighter as the sweating men bulled it into place. Wood squealed against wood as the section mated with the base plate.

One of the men bellowed, "Wait—stop! There ain't nothin' to hold this thing in place—it'll just—"

"Shaddup an' push," another voice growled. "We almost got 'er!"

"But look! There ain't nothin'—"

"Push!"

The section, almost upright, wavered like a newborn foal trying out its legs—and then it was in place. A cheer went up from the men. The section stood square and straight and perfectly in place—for perhaps three seconds. Then, slowly, inexorably, it began to tip into the interior of the church, building speed and momentum as it fell. The crash of wood against the newly laid floor was like that of an artillery piece. John Stiles flinched at the racket at the same moment he stepped over the edge of the choir stage, flinging his arms out to his sides with a startled, feminine shriek. The beam slammed to— and through—the freshly varnished surface of the small stage. John sprawled on his back onto the table holding the water barrel and the sandwiches and pies and cakes the ladies of the congregation had provided. The table, of course, collapsed under his weight.

Directly outside, Davey Pestle's team of young mules bolted at the noise, their eyes bulging. The load of bricks they hauled in a wagon erupted into the air as the mules raced across the rutted and rocky field adjacent to the church site. Davey, his face scarlet, opened his mouth to shout at his team and then closed it, remembering where he was. He gaped silently as his wagon launched itself into the air, overturned, and splintered on the ground. The harness leathers parted as easily as over- cooked noodles, and the mules galloped off in separate directions.

Lee tugged her Stetson off and swatted Ben with it. "There's nothing funny about that," she snapped.

Ben shifted Snorty out of striking range, tears of laughter forming in his eyes. "Everything's funny about that," he gasped.

36

Lee edged her horse closer to him and whacked him again with her hat. Then the corners of her mouth quivered slightly as she struggled to contain her own laughter. For a moment she was successful—and then her giggles escaped. When the couple looked again toward the building, John Stiles and Davey Pestle stood side by side, glaring at them. The side of John's head was thickly coated with chocolate frosting.

"We'd better get outta here," Ben whispered, turning Snorty toward town. Lee smiled at John for another second, then hustled her old mount into a shuffling semblance of a gallop.

As they rode together down Main Street, Lee marveled at how the town was growing. The church was nearing completion, and although the majority of the work had been done by volunteers, the building would soon be completely closed in and roofed. Lyle Zempner, a carpenter and a recent convert, had donated his skills, time, and materials, and more than half the pews were already in place, covered with heavy tarps and awaiting the completion of the roof.

The two massive stained glass windows Missy had ordered from a church supply house in Rochester, New York, hadn't arrived yet but were due within a few days. The congregation had wisely drafted Lyle Zempner and his assistants to install the precious windows.

Main Street bustled with Saturday shoppers as Ben and Lee stopped in front of O'Keefe's Café. "You go ahead an' order up a coffee for me an' whatever you want, Lee," Ben said. "I'll go down to the post office and collect the mail."

Lee grinned. "Just coffee?"

"A good, thick slice of apple pie would go real good with that coffee. But you're the one who says I'm developin' a belly. Make up your mind, ma'am."

When Ben strode into the café a few minutes later, Lee was at a table, forking a bite of rhubarb pie into her mouth.

"Couldn't wait for me, huh?" he commented. He set a half dozen envelopes on the table in front of her and sat down, his back to the rear wall. Waiting for him were a mug of steaming black coffee and a very generous triangle of apple pie.

"Bessie's outdone herself with this pie," Lee said with a smile. "No way in the world could I sit here and look at it and smell it without trying it." She sorted through the envelopes for a moment, selected one, and used her thumbnail to open it. After reading the first couple of lines, she sighed, quoting for Ben, "'I regret that I feel my ministry would more effectively serve the Lord in a venue more expansive than that of your fine town.'"

"Translated: 'I ain't comin' to a dust hole in the middle of Texas for $1,300 a year.'"

Lee opened another letter and again quoted, "'I fear I need to be where the climate would be more salubrious, since I suffer allergies and am prone to chills.'"

"We're hotter'n Gehenna in the summer an' freezin' cold all winter, is what he's sayin'," Ben grumbled.

Lee nodded. She slit the top of the next envelope and scanned the letter. She sat up straight in her chair. "Hey . . ." she said quietly.

Ben held his curiosity until she'd finished reading the letter. When she looked up at him, she was smiling.

"This fellow's name is Duncan Warner," she said. She lowered her eyes to the letter once again. "He graduated from the Medina School of Theology with high honors, and he's assisted at a couple of churches—one in Kansas and one in Oklahoma. He's forty-four years old, single,

38

favors a strict interpretation of Scripture, and he's looking for a church of his own. He's willing to accept the salary—says money's not important to him, but serving God is. Let's see . . . he didn't go directly into ministry after his graduation because he had to care for his mother, who died after a prolonged illness. He's preached at some revivals . . ." She refolded the letter carefully. "He sounds good to me, Ben."

"Where's Medina?"

"Doesn't say—probably a small divinity school in the East somewhere. He certainly sounds enthusiastic enough, and I like the fact that he tended to his mother until her death." Her eyes glinted. "He might work out perfectly. What do you think?"

Ben sipped his coffee before answering. "Well, it ain't like we're swamped with offers to come here. Duncan Warner sounds fine on paper. Let's present him to the board tonight and see if we can squeeze some travel money out of the church fund. Can't hurt to bring him here an' see what he has to say for himself."

"You sound dubious, Ben."

"I'm not—maybe just careful. It seems like you've got him hired an' preachin' his first sermon already. Could be Burnt Rock'll scare him right back to Medina. That's all I'm sayin'. I don't want you to get your hopes all up and then have the man turn out to be wrong for us."

"He's not in Medina now—that's where he went to school. He's in Chicago. I know what you mean, of course. But this is the first positive response we've gotten to that ton of letters I sent out. I suppose I might sound like I'm ready to hire anyone tall enough to be seen behind the pulpit, but I'm really not. The waiting's frustrating, though."

"We don't even *have* a pulpit yet." He smiled to soften the words.

"I know that." She returned his smile, if a bit ruefully. "It just seems like everything's going so slowly. I expected that we'd have at least a few candidate ministers to choose from, and we're way behind on the building schedule we figured out—"

"But you gotta realize that most of the men involved in the building don't know all that much about carpentry. Most of us can whack together a chicken coop or a lean-to for a horse, but that's about it. That schedule we worked out would probably give a real builder a laugh— I know Lyle had one when he looked at it. And like it or not, Burnt Rock is a little burg in the middle of nowhere that doesn't have a whole lot to offer a man of God— 'specially a young fella who's bound an' determined to light the world on fire and bring every man, woman, and child to the Lord. It's only natural that those young fellas want to be where there's lots of people to do their ministering to."

"But we do have something every minister needs, regardless of his age."

"What's that?"

"We have a growing number of believers who need a leader and a teacher." She paused for a moment, and then her smile returned. "Maybe this Duncan Warner fellow is the answer to our prayers. Maybe his calling doesn't send him to big cities and masses of people. That's possible, you know."

Ben thought for a moment. "Of course, it's possible," he said, forcing more enthusiasm into his voice than he felt. "You're right—I need to put more faith in the fact that the Lord will help us. Maybe I need to spend more time on my knees and less time complaining."

"Couldn't hurt, now, could it?" She reached over and squeezed his hand.

Lee had a special place on the Busted Thumb Horse Farm that she sought out when she needed to be alone, when she was confused or concerned, or when she simply wanted to reflect on and give thanks for the blessings God had given her. The land beyond the two barns—the large one housing horses and hay and tack, the smaller housing stalls for ill or injured horses and mares nearing motherhood—sloped gently uphill. Atop a grade a mile from her house, she had found a cluster of desert pines and a series of boulders that offered flattened surfaces to sit on. A year ago she'd taken Ben there for the first time.

This night, after a meal with Carlos and Maria, Ben and Lee sought fresh air and a time to talk. The night was dark but there was a half moon, and the stars glittered above them like diamonds tossed from the hand of God. As the couple walked, their hands found one another easily, comfortably, and neither Ben nor Lee said much as they meandered up the hill. The air was sweet and carried the aroma of buffalo grass. When they stood on the plateau at the top of the rise, they gazed down on the barns and the two frame houses—Lee's and, across the corral, Carlos and Maria's—for several minutes.

When Ben put his hand gently on Lee's shoulder to turn her to him, she moved closer. They kissed silently, lovingly. After a few moments, Lee stepped back. "Let's sit on the big rock," she said. "I have some things I need to say."

"Sounds serious."

"It's just some things that've been on my mind."

41

A boulder with a wide, flat top still held some remnants of the day's heat. They sat side by side, shoulders touching, hands again together.

Lee cleared her throat before speaking. "We've known each other for over four years, Ben."

"An' those four years have been the best and sweetest ones of my life," he replied. "You know that. I . . . I don't know what I'd do without you in my life. I really don't."

"I feel the same way about you. The thing is, I sometimes wonder what things are going to be like for us in five years—or fifteen. This—what we have—is good. But I . . . oh, I don't know."

"We'll be together if I have any say in it, just like we are now."

"Well, that's what I'm talking about," Lee said. "I just wonder if there should be more to our lives together than dinner a couple of times a week and some church meetings and Bible studies." She sighed. "You'll ride back to Burnt Rock tonight, and I'll be here."

For the first time since he'd quit smoking almost six years ago, Ben craved a cigarette. He could almost feel the satiny surface of a leaf of rolling paper between his fingers and smell the heady aroma of burning tobacco. "What are you saying?" he asked quietly.

For a long moment, Lee didn't reply. She cleared her throat again and at the same time gently removed her hand from his. "I wish I could tell you, but I'm not even completely sure myself. At times I wonder . . . well . . . maybe I wonder about the future a bit."

It was his turn to clear his throat. "I see."

"*You see?* Is that all you can say? Don't you feel any of what I'm feeling?"

"Of course I do, Lee. I love you more than I thought I could ever love another person. You're more important to me than air and food and water and anything else in the world. The fact of it is, I love you with all my heart an' all that I am or ever can be."

"Then what—"

"You need to hear me out," he interrupted. "Look . . ." Suddenly he was without words. He rose from the boulder and stood in front of her, his hands hanging self-consciously at his sides. The tips of his right fingers brushed the bone grips of the Colt in its holster. "I'm not real sure how to say this."

"Just say it, whatever it is. I want—I need—to hear it."

"OK. I'll do that. When I stood up a second ago, my fingers automatically checked to make sure my pistol was where it's supposed to be. I carry a gun, Lee, an' I've carried one weapon or another for a lot of years. I was maybe sixteen when I first strapped on a gun, an' I've never taken it off since."

"It's your job. You're a lawman."

"That ain't what I mean. What I'm sayin' is that I've led a violent life, an' guns an' fighting an' bloodshed an' death have always been part of it. The things I did at Shiloh and Gettysburg and near the end at Richmond were ungodly and evil and horrible, and they tainted me. They changed me. They marked me and made me into . . . I dunno . . . some kinda machine. I guess it's like the rider we read about in Revelations who brought death wherever he and his three partners went." His voice broke. "I don't want to bring hurt to you."

Lee's voice was soft and slightly husky. "Do you really think that's what would happen if we shared our lives?"

Keeping his eyes on the ground, he shook his head. "I don't know. But it scares me."

43

"War is a hideous, hateful thing. But the War Between the States is over." Her voice strengthened and became a bit louder. "Ben—I do love you, and I need to say this: Maybe it's time for you to come home from Shiloh and Gettysburg."

His right hand began to move upward to her shoulder, then dropped to his side. His voice was lower when he spoke again. "Remember the day Rev was killed an' you and me were in my office an' Missy Joplin' came bullin' through the door like she always does? Do you remember that?"

"Of course I remember it. She startled both of us, and you . . ."

"And I what? And I *drew* on her, Lee. That's what I did, and I did it from instinct, just like a snake strikes out at an enemy out of instinct."

"But Ben—"

He waved off her words. "An' suppose I was standin' in our kitchen an' you dropped a dish or somethin' an' it smashed on the floor an' my nerves was tight that day for some reason an'. . ." He took a breath. "And there's this, Lee—my job is to face drunks and drifters and outlaws who hate everyone else as much as they hate themselves. One day I could come up against a man who's a little luckier or a little faster than I am. Or a coward with a buffalo rifle could drop me from a half mile away. Then what would you have as my wife? A husband shot fulla holes who doesn't even own a suit to be buried in, and no one to take care of you."

"But Ben, I don't need anyone to take care of me. You know that. I own a horse ranch and I breed the best horses in Texas. I've been able to look after myself almost my whole life, and I've done a good job of it. It's a man's world out here on the frontier, but I never let that slow

me down, much less stop me. I don't want a caretaker—
I want Ben Flood to be my husband and my life-partner."
She turned away quickly, as if to hide the tears that were
flooding her eyes.

Ben stepped back. He felt as if he'd just taken an unexpected punch to the gut. "Lee," he said, "I didn't mean
it that way. I understand your independence and grit—
it's a big part of what makes me love you. Remember
when you rode Slick in that race? I was so proud I
could've busted wide open with it." His words came
faster now, tumbling over one another. "I wouldn't want
anythin' about you to change. I didn't mean what it
sounded like. You gotta believe me. I never met a woman
like you before, an' I thank the Lord for each minute I
have with you."

Lee used the back of her hand to dry her eyes as she
turned toward him. "You came to the Lord years ago,
but it seems like you haven't heard a word that's been
said about forgiveness, Ben. What it sounds like to me
is that you believe that even though God forgives you
for what happened earlier in your life, you need to
carry all your guilt in your heart and in your mind forever."

Ben clenched his fists. "I was talking about my
work, my job, and what it'd mean to us in our lives
together. About how I've lived my life and who and
what I am."

"There are other jobs. Lots of them. You're a fine
horseman. You could train at the Busted Thumb. Or you
could do whatever else you want to do. I don't care—I
really don't."

He swallowed his first response and held himself in
check for a moment. When he spoke, his voice was con-
ciliatory. "Wouldn't work, Lee. I'm real good at what I

do. I'm the best lawman Burnt Rock has ever had, and that job is what I want to do. It's part of who I am—how I see things." He swallowed hard. "Look here, Lee—I'd never ask you to give up bein' who you are for me, and I'd never ask you to give up the Busted Thumb. Maybe me bein' a lawman is like you bein' a rancher."

Lee seemed to slump into herself, as if her bones had lost their strength and could no longer carry her weight. "We've needed to say these things. It was important for you to hear what I said, and I needed to hear what you said." She paused. "Let's go back. It's cold up here."

"Not before I say this again: I love you, Lee Morgan."

She sighed and swiped at her eyes. Ben moved in front of her. They stood facing each other for what seemed like a very long time. The breeze ruffled through the trees and rattled the stalks of dead buffalo grass as it swept past. The other night sounds were strangely hushed.

"Lee . . ." Ben's voice was tentative and weighed with sadness. He reached out for her, but she was already moving toward him, a sound escaping from her that made tears spring to his eyes. They embraced urgently, as if not to do so was unthinkable, impossible. He felt her heart beating against his chest.

The X-Bar Cattle Company hit Burnt Rock the next morning with eight hundred head of Texas longhorn stock, most of which had lived their lives on thousands of acres of open pasture, not having seen a human being since the day they were branded. Even seven weeks on the trail hadn't acclimated them to being moved by men on horses. Longhorns by nature weren't tractable animals. They seemed to be born with the temperament of angry hornets, and they were difficult and dangerous to

46

be around. The expanse of their horns—a four-foot spread wasn't at all unusual—took a bloody toll of good horses every year, and during many drives at least one wrangler's body was buried in the sandy dirt of the prairie, with a wooden marker that wouldn't last through the winter.

There seemed to be only one difference between the cowboys and the longhorns they herded: The men walked upright. The X-Bar cowboys filled Ben's four cells and kept them filled with double and triple occupancy for a week or so after the cattle were penned at the railroad junction.

Ben sat behind his desk, red-eyed and weary. There was a purple-and-yellow bruise just under his left eye, and his nose was swollen to a grotesque mass that was more than a little off-center on his face. He sipped at his coffee and cringed when the hot liquid touched his split lower lip. He grunted in pain and looked down at the ledger in front of him, reviewing the list of the crimes for which the X-Bar cowboys had been arrested.

Misdemeanor	Name	Fine/Sentence
Discharging weapon in mercantile	Myers	$5/5 days
Fistfight	Hamm/Torpey	$5/1 day
Fistfight	Hamm/Torpey	$10/3 days
Roping chicken on Main Street	Hogan	$5/no time
Riding horse into millenery	Vasquez	$5/no time
Public intoxication	Marini	$5/1 day
Roping banker	Drumm	$10/2 days
Bathing in horse trough—public nudity	Wilson	$10/2 days
Theft of beer wagon	Various	$70/no time
Consumption of contents	Various	(too many to hold)
Horse racing on Main Street	Stapp/Franken	$10/no time

47

Ben began to turn to the next page of offenses, sighed, and then closed the ledger. He was lifting his coffee mug to his mouth when Lee walked in from the street.

"Oh, Ben! You look terrible!" She closed the office door behind her and hurried to his desk. "What happened? Are you all right?"

He forced a feeble grin. "The X-Bar crew is what happened. Nothin' serious. Some of the boys get a little silly at the end of a drive, that's all."

Lee touched a tentative finger to the bruise under his eye. "I'll fetch Doc. He should have a look at this, and at your poor nose."

"Don't do that. I'm fine. Doc's more of a mother hen than you are. He'll paste me up with that stuff that smells like udder balm. I'm fine—just a little banged up is all."

Lee stepped back from the desk. "A little banged up?"

Ben stood from his chair, not completely masking the grimace of pain that crossed his face as he did so. "Those guys are the best cowhands I've ever seen. Kurt, the young kid with the flashy buckskin gelding, roped a running hen from that good horse of his without disturbing a feather on her. It was somethin' to see."

"But Ben, I heard all about that. The poor bird will probably never lay another egg in her life! And where did those hooligans get the chickens to rope?"

"Well . . . Kurt and his partner kinda opened a crate on a freight wagon. But they paid for the chickens later."

Lee crossed her arms over her chest. "It sounds to me like you're justifying what a bunch of drunken fools do to Burnt Rock every year, Ben, and that's not right."

Ben sighed, picked up his mug, and walked to the coffeepot on the potbelly stove across the room. "The boys raise some dust," he admitted. "But there's no meanness to it. If I'd been doin' what they have for the past couple of months and eatin' chuck wagon grub every day, I might do some whoopin' myself when I hit civilization."

Lee looked at him appraisingly. When the slightest sign of a grin appeared on her face, she turned to the door. "I don't doubt that you would," she said. "But if there's no meanness in those crazies, what happened to your face?"

"I kinda got between a couple fellas named Hamm and Torpey who were arguin' about politics is all. They—"

"All right, I see what you mean," she protested, holding up her hands. "Listen, I'm going for the mail. Meet me at O'Keefe's in a few minutes." She eyed his coffeepot. "At least the coffee is drinkable there."

She closed the door more strongly than she needed to. Ben watched some papers flutter to the floor. He sighed again.

Only a few of the regulars were in O'Keefe's. The morning crowd had long since left, and it was too early for lunch. The lingerers—and Bessie—greeted Ben as usual. He noticed that everyone kept their eyes from his face as they spoke to him, jacking up his self-consciousness about his battered appearance at least another notch. He took a rear table where he could sit with his back to the wall and asked Bessie for a couple cups of coffee.

A moment later, Lee hustled into the restaurant, her chestnut eyes snapping as she sat in the chair across from him and tore open the envelope she'd carried into the café. "It's from Duncan Warner," she said.

Bessie brought the coffee and then stood next to the table, waiting for Lee to read the letter. Lee wasn't much for whooping in public places, but today she made an exception.

49

"He's coming to Burnt Rock!" she hollered. "Reverend Warner is coming to Burnt Rock to meet with us about the job!"

Bessie squealed, and a wide smile spread across Ben's face, even though it hurt more than a little bit. "That's great," he said. "When will he be here?"

Lee read the rest of the letter quickly. "About three weeks, depending on the train and stage schedule. He'll wire us when he's a couple of days out. He doesn't say much else—just that he's prayed about our church and believes the Lord has directed him here. He says he's closing up his affairs in Chicago. If we like him, he'll stay here, and if not, he'll move on to another town that's interested in him."

"This could be so good for us," Bessie said, almost bouncing up and down as she spoke. "Thank the Lord, we may finally have a preacher in town!"

But Ben merely sipped his coffee. *All the others begged off in a hurry. This fella seems awful anxious—maybe too anxious.* He tried to join in Lee and Bessie's happiness, but only his mouth smiled. His eyes didn't.

4

Missy Joplin had her teeth in, and it wasn't even Sunday.

Lee stood next to her elderly friend, the pair of them waiting on the wooden sidewalk in front of the Wells Fargo depot to welcome Duncan Warner. Both women were dressed in their Sunday finest, and each wore a large sunhat. The midday sun pounded down on them, but not with the unrelenting power it had possessed in the heart of the summer. Now that August was in its final days, the white-hot fist that had clutched West Texas since early May slowly was releasing its grasp. A vagrant breeze meandered through town, putting dust and grit into the air when it touched the rutted dirt of Main Street. Ben stood waiting off to the side, his arms folded across his chest, his eyes in a continuous sweep about his town.

When a small chimera of dust appeared to the east of Burnt Rock, Lee said almost breathlessly, "That's the stage!" Ben unfolded his arms and moved a couple of steps forward, closer to the two women.

The four-passenger stagecoach clattered down Main Street toward the depot, the side curtains of the passenger compartment closed against the sun and dust. The six horses were sweating but not lathered, and the leather suspension of the coach and the dry wood of the frame squeaked and groaned under the weight of the passengers and the wooden crates strapped to the top. The driver, a gnarled, middle-aged man with a face like a tumbleweed, pulled the stage to a halt in the middle of the street. The shotgun rider next to him stood and rubbed his lower back with his left hand, his double-barreled Remington twelve-gauge clutched in his right. The horses blew and snorted, knowing they'd soon have the water and feed they craved.

When the passenger compartment door swung open, a young cowhand with a stock saddle slung over his shoulder stepped down from the coach. His face reddened, most likely with embarrassment at being in the unexpected presence of two such finely dressed ladies and a man with a star on his chest. He managed a friendly wave but didn't waste any time getting on down the street.

Reverend Duncan Warner stepped down from the coach gracefully, a leather valise in his left hand. The valise looked brand new, its leather polished, as if the preacher had purchased it just for this trip. The man stood at Ben's height—about two inches over six feet—and was dressed in a dark suit that fit him too well to have been ordered from a Montgomery Ward catalog. He looked his stated forty-four years of age, and his skin had the deep color of a man who spent a good amount of time outdoors. His features were even—handsome, actually—and when he smiled his teeth were straight and white against his tanned face. He looked fresh, even after a long ride in a stifling stagecoach.

Lee and Missy stepped toward him. "I'm Reverend Warner," he said before either of the ladies could speak. "Duncan Warner. I'm very glad to be here." Then he grinned and added, "If you ladies aren't here to meet me, I guess I'm getting off at the wrong stop. But assuming you are, I'm pleased to meet you."

Ben noticed that Rev Warner's voice projected like one very accustomed to speaking to audiences—rich, deep, his elocution flawless. He watched as Lee and Missy stepped forward and stood in front of the preacher.

Lee cleared her throat. "On behalf of Burnt Rock, we're pleased to welcome you to our town. I'm Lee Morgan. I'm the one who wrote to you."

Missy smiled and extended her hand. "I'm Hannah Joplin," she said, "but everyone calls me Missy. I'd be pleased if you would too."

Warner bowed the slightest bit as he took Missy's hand. "I'll do just that, Missy. Thank you." He released her hand and reached for Lee's. "You write a fine and legible letter, Miss Morgan. You must have paid close attention to penmanship and composition in school."

Lee's cheeks reddened. "Why, thank you, Reverend Warner."

Ben stepped up, and Lee turned to him. "This is Marshall Benjamin Flood. He's the law in Burnt Rock."

The two men shook hands. "Good to meet you, Mr. Flood," the preacher said, smiling. "I hope to stay on your good side as long as I'm in Burnt Rock—no matter how long or short a time that may be."

"Pleased to meet you too, Reverend," Ben said. "I wish some of the cattle crews and cowhands who show up in

53

town would give me the same greeting. Things would be a lot quieter." He noticed that the preacher's palm felt hard and dry, and that there was strength in his fingers. *Strange. Turning the pages of a Bible doesn't callus a man's hand.*

Warner chuckled politely. "I'm sure you're able to keep matters well in hand, Mr. Flood."

"Please, call me Ben. We're not awful formal round here."

"I'd be glad to. I'm no friend of needless formality either. Please—all of you—call me either Rev or Duncan. 'Reverend Warner' makes me feel self-conscious, as if I set myself apart in some way from others. That's not the case at all. If nothing else, I'm a man of the people. The Lord has chosen to work through me, but that's to his glory, certainly not to mine."

Missy beamed at him, obviously pleased with his words. "You must be starved, Rev," she said brightly. "Let's go on down to the café and we'll see to that. We've got a nice room for you at the hotel, and after we eat you can go and rest up from your trip."

"Fine, fine," Warner said. "Now—as to the arrangements . . . ?"

Lee looked confused for a moment. "Arrangements?" Then she smiled. "I'm sorry, Rev. Of course, you want to know what's going to happen in terms of the church board. I'm afraid the quickest we can meet isn't until next Wednesday. One of our members is out of town until then, and another is down with ague. I know that's almost a week away, but it's the best we could do."

"Well," Warner said. His voice was the least bit less expansive and warm. "Frankly, I anticipated the meeting and interview to take place on a more expeditious basis. You see . . . there's another church that . . . no, never mind that. I can wire them. And I'll have the interim time here in Burnt Rock to meet a few people and get to know a bit about the town. Perhaps the slight delay is a blessing in disguise." He smiled broadly, announcing the matter to be closed. "Now, then—did someone mention a meal? The food at the stage stop early this morning was atrocious—and it was a long time ago!"

Lee wondered if any of the chairs in the café had ever before been pulled out for ladies in the manner Reverend Warner did it for her and Missy. Ben would often tug a chair away from the table for her, but it tended to look like an afterthought, something he'd almost forgotten to do. The preacher, however, moved the chairs as if it were his particular honor to do so, and he met and held her eyes as she sat.

Bessie served them, but her usual bantering with Lee, Ben, and Missy was replaced by a stiff formality, and her customary "Can I get you anything else?" became "Will there be anything further?" Lee smiled inwardly. The Reverend seemed to be the sort of man who garnered respect and even preferential treatment from people everywhere he went. Was that, she wondered, because he was a man of God or because of his manners? This time a smile reached her face. *Or is it because he looks like the hero of a stage play?*

"Something funny, Lee?" Ben asked. "You're grinnin' like a kid at Christmas."

"I'm just glad we're all here and that we're finally meeting."

"No more pleased than I am," Warner said, patting lightly at his mouth with a napkin.

"Letters are fine for what they are," Missy piped up. "But I don't think they're a measure of a person. Takes a real settin' down together like we're doin' to get a feel 'bout someone. Now, Rev Warner here, I can tell he's—"

A prolonged whoop from the street, followed by the pounding of hooves, interrupted Missy's speech. Ben stood up suddenly, as if he'd been waiting for the moment. Lee glanced toward the street through the front window of the café. The Benson twins—nine-year-old boys—rode by double on their dad's carriage horse, both wearing Indian headdresses made from chicken feathers.

"I gotta check on that," Ben said, grabbing his hat. "Sorry, Rev. Ladies."

Lee caught the hardness of his eyes before he turned away. "It was only the . . ." she began, but Ben was already halfway across the room.

"His must be a trying job," Warner observed. After a moment, he added, "Tell me more about the people of your church, ladies. I'm very much looking forward to getting to know them."

Reverend Duncan Warner had plenty of time to think over the next six days. The rain that fostered bountiful crops and fat cattle and horses had begun as he, Missy, and Lee had left O'Keefe's Café, and it hadn't let up in four days. It wasn't a driving rain, but it made walking about town decidedly uncomfortable, and since not all of Main Street had sidewalks, the viscous mud played havoc on well-shined shoes.

Warner stepped away from the window facing the street and slumped into the single chair his room at the Merchant's Rest Hotel provided. *An interesting little town,* he thought. *Rich with opportunity for the right preacher.* As he shifted uncomfortably in the chair, the harsh light of the lamp on the dresser seemed to drive itself into his eyes. *The waiting is the hardest part for a man with a mission.*

The preacher walked the few steps to the coffin-sized closet. He sorted through his two suits, several pairs of trousers, and a series of starched white shirts and found what he was after: a shawl-like cloak that would keep the rain off his shoulders, chest, and back. A pair of mud-encrusted shoes rested forlornly near the door. He pulled them on, buttoned them, and stepped out of his room, locking the door behind him.

The tinkling of the piano from the Drovers' Inn is an oddly light and innocent sound to issue from such a den of iniquity, he thought. It seemed to call to him. He turned in the opposite direction as he began his walk. The wind had picked up since the afternoon, and it was now blowing the rain in gusts. The preacher looked up and down Main Street. All the shops and stores had long since been closed for the night, and the only lights shone from the saloon, the livery stable, and the marshall's office. *A hard man, that Ben Flood. Not one to trust another quickly, and guarded about himself. Proprietary toward Lee Morgan too.*

A sheet of rain began down the deserted street, and the preacher stepped into the alley beside Scott's Mercantile to avoid it. A creaking sound down the alley caught his attention. As he watched in the murky darkness, a slight form clutching something to its chest backed out of a side door to the mercantile. As clouds shifted away from the moon, Warner saw that the figure's movements were quick and furtive.

"Hey!" he said.

The boy—Warner could now see it was a boy—spun and bolted, flinging away what he was carrying. The slick mud was treacherous, and the boy's boots skidded out from under him. He went down in the muck. Before the boy could scramble to his feet, Warner had a good hold of his arm and the back of his neck.

"What's this all about?" Warner demanded.

"Lemme go! I didn't do nothin'!"

"You broke into this store and were stealing from it. That sounds like something to me. Who are you?"

"You can go right to—"

Warner released the boy's arm and with the same hand slapped him sharply across the face, cutting off the curse. The boy cowered back against the wall, his eyes wide in fear. Rain drained from the narrow brim of his oversized bowler onto his shoulders, chest, and back. Warner saw he was dressed in rags.

"There's no call for cursing. What's your name, son?"

"Henry. Jus' Henry. I got no last name."

"Where do you live, Henry? Where are your parents?" He eased his hand free of the boy's neck but stood directly in front of the cowering youth, blocking his escape.

"I been stayin' at the smithy shop. The owner lets me sleep there if I clean up the place each day. I ain't got no parents." The thief's spirit seemed to be returning. "What's it to ya, anyway? If you're gonna take me to the marshall, let's get goin'. Least I'll sleep dry an' on a cot tonight."

Warner chuckled. "Why'd you do this, son? Why'd you break into the store?"

"Why's anybody steal? I needed some stuff, an' I didn't have any money."

Warner turned his head to the side for a moment. An Armor's canned ham was submerged in mud, and a blanket was soaking up rain where it had landed.

"You'd risk jail for things worth a couple of dollars?"

"Look, Mister—I ain't gonna stand here an' jaw with you. Either take me to Flood's office or leave me alone."

Warner thought for a moment. When he spoke, the sharpness was gone from his voice. "I don't think I'm going to turn you in, Henry. I think that maybe we can be friends. I'm going to be the new preacher here, and I could use a friend. Are you a believer, son?"

"I dunno. I lived for a bit with some folks who had religion. I guess I didn't take to it. Hey, you bein' straight about not takin' me in?"

"I am. Perhaps we can both use a friend. Take the blanket and the ham and go on your way. Being hungry is no sin. But don't let me learn of you breaking into another store, you hear me?"

"Yeah. I hear."

"After I'm installed at the church, we'll talk again—we'll talk about many things. Is that all right with you?"

"I guess so, if that's what you want. I ain't much for talkin', though."

Warner stepped back and held out his hand. Henry paused and then shook it. "One thing," the boy said. "Don't you never hit me again."

"Don't give me a reason to, Henry." The preacher smiled. "I'm looking forward to our talks. Bless you, son."

The rain stopped the afternoon before the meeting, but the air remained thick with humidity. The six members of the Burnt Rock church board sat on either side of a long table in the meeting room of Grange Hall. It was brighter than day due to the three large lamps suspended from the ceiling, and although the room's single window was open, no air stirred.

Lee, Missy, and Sam Turner sat on one side of the table, and Joshua Scott, Harvey Stein and his wife, Rose, and Deland Ehrich, the photographer, sat on the other.

59

All were dressed as if for an important occasion—which this meeting was.

Duncan Warner, standing at the head of the table, had kept his initial presentation short, citing his education at the School of Theology in Medina, New York, and his work as assistant pastor at three small churches afterward. He responded to scriptural questions from the board like a biblical scholar, stressing his strict interpretation of the Word of God. Then, he closed.

"These are letters from each of the pastors I worked under," he said, taking three envelopes from the inner pocket of his suit coat and placing them on the table. "I'll ask you to read them. I think you'll find them quite complimentary concerning my work."

"What exactly was your work in Chicago, Reverend Warner?" Sam Turner asked.

The preacher paused and looked down at the table. "My mission there was a difficult one," he answered. "And it was one at which I failed."

The board members waited, their eyes locked on Warner's face. For a long moment, the preacher said nothing. When he looked up from the table, his face seemed to have lost some of its healthy glow. A bead of sweat started at his hairline and ran down his cheek. "Because of the ladies present, I hesitate to expand on the subject," he said quietly.

"We're brothers and sisters in Christ here, Reverend," Missy said. "You needn't be embarrassed. Please go on."

Warner straightened his shoulders. "Very well. Chicago is a city given to sins of the flesh. My mission—and it was one I assigned to myself—was to work with the soiled doves who offered their bodies to men for money. These fallen women live lives of terrible degradation, of calamitous sin, of utter godlessness. I believed that I heard their silent voices crying out for the Lord even as they went about their licentious business. I worked with them, counseled them, brought them the words of God. My eyes have seen horrors that I'll never forget, ladies and gentlemen. I did all I possibly could for those women. They spurned me, laughed at me, ridiculed me and what I was trying to do for them and with them. Then their men turned on me—not only their customers but the owners of the brothels." He pushed aside his collar, revealing a slightly raised pale scar the size of a five-cent piece on the fleshy part of his neck. "This was from a bullet," he said quietly. "I have scars from the lash on my back and chest."

There was an audible intake of breath by the board members.

"When I was finally able to leave the hospital, I prayed for counsel. I knew I had failed the Lord, and I asked that he provide another chance for me, another opportunity to spread his Word and work with his people." He sighed. "That's why I'm here."

"One further question," Mrs. Stein said. "What was it that brought you to take on such an impossible task?"

The preacher leaned forward and put both of his hands on the table, almost supporting himself with them. He lowered his head. When he spoke, his voice was tortured. "My younger sister, Emma, had become a prostitute. She died of a wasting disease in an alley in Chicago."

Deland Ehrich cleared his throat and met the eyes of each of his fellow board members individually, turning his head slowly. "Thank you, Reverend Warner. I'll now ask you to leave the room for a few moments." He cleared his throat again and added, "I don't think we'll be long."

5

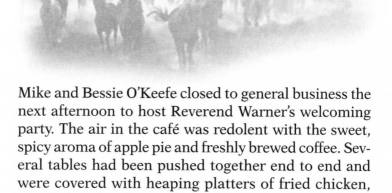

Mike and Bessie O'Keefe closed to general business the next afternoon to host Reverend Warner's welcoming party. The air in the café was redolent with the sweet, spicy aroma of apple pie and freshly brewed coffee. Several tables had been pushed together end to end and were covered with heaping platters of fried chicken, sliced roast beef, sugar-coated ham, bowls mounded with thick, creamy mashed potatoes, a large tureen of vegetable soup, rolls and bread still warm from the oven, and several quart crocks of fresh butter. The children had been let out of school early for the celebration, and Bessie put them to work cranking the ice cream maker.

Rev Warner stood at the head of a receiving line after everyone had eaten, flanked by Missy and Lee. Many of the older ladies in his flock fussed over him, and more than a few had tears in their eyes as they welcomed their new shepherd. Sam Turner discreetly handed Warner an envelope, as did several of the other wealthy cattle-men and merchants of the town. When the line finally ended, the preacher had a half dozen envelopes in his hand as he addressed the group.

"I thank the good folks who handed these to me," he said, holding the envelopes up. "My cup runneth over. But, my good people, you've already provided me with a church and a home, and Mr. O'Keefe has offered to supply me with his and Bessie's wonderful food. I have no need for money. I'm sure that there are people in our congregation who can put these generous offerings to good use for food or medicine or whatever it is they lack and cannot afford. I'm going to call upon Marshall Flood to administer this money as he sees fit. As the lawman in town, he sees both the good and the bad, the wealthy and the needy, the joy and the suffering, and he'll know best where the funds are needed the most." He motioned to Ben. "Will you do that for us, Marshall? Could you step up here for a moment, please?"

Ben, standing next to Carlos and Maria, remained in place until Maria nudged him forward toward where the preacher was waiting. Ben walked stiffly ahead, not at all comfortable. When he stood next to the preacher to accept the envelopes, the contrast between the two men was glaringly apparent. Rev Warner was at ease, casual but alert. Ben's hands hung at his sides awkwardly; he had no idea what to do with them.

"I, uhh . . . thanks, Reverend Warner. I'll try to give this money to the nost meedy—uhh . . . most needy. And I . . . uhh . . ." Ben's voice and the thought died together. His eyes found Lee's, and she smiled at him.

The preacher handed the envelopes to Ben, who accepted them with a damp right hand. "I'm sure you will, Marshall," Warner said. "And I thank you for your—"

The sharp bark of a rifle shot filled the café like an unanticipated burst of thunder. Ben released the envelopes, and his right hand swooped down to his holstered Colt .45. In less than a second, the weapon was in his hand and he was dashing toward the door. Out of the corner of his eye, he saw Rev Warner's right shoulder dip as his hand darted to his own right side.

In front of Scott's Mercantile, next to the café, a young boy stood gawking at a lever-action Winchester 30.06 rifle in the dirt at his feet, next to a farm wagon with a pair of mules tied to the hitching post. The youngster's eyes were wide with fear, and his face was moon-pale. Ben holstered his pistol and quickly strode toward the boy. He stopped, glaring down at the frightened youth, whose eyes were glistening with tears.

"I didn't mean for it to go off, Marshall. I promise I didn't! I was jist gonna look at it an' hold it is all. Then when I was pullin' it out from under the seat, I dropped it an' it went off. I didn't mean nothin', Marshall Flood."

"Doesn't much matter what you meant or didn't mean, Wilbert," Ben said. "A slug kills a person just as dead whether you mean to kill him or not." He paused for a moment, holding the boy's gaze. "Did you work the lever, boy? Cock the rifle?"

"Nossir. I promise I didn't."

"I believe you, Wilbert. When you dropped the rifle, the butt hit the ground first, right?"

"Yessir. That's when it went off."

Ben crouched down, putting himself at eye level with the boy. "You know you could have killed someone today? Maybe somebody walking by or maybe some-

64

body inside the café? Maybe one of the kids you go to school with? How do you think you'd feel then?"

"I . . . I'd be awful sad an' sorry, Marshall," the boy said, his voice a constricted whisper.

"Guns aren't toys, Wilbert. They're as deadly as a sack of rattlesnakes. You understand that?"

"Yessir. I surely do."

"Now, I need a promise from you. I want you to raise your right hand and promise you'll never fool around with guns again till you're a grown man or till you have a good man teachin' you about them. Go on, boy—raise your hand and say that promise."

Wilbert complied, his voice barely audible through his tears. Then Ben stood and put his hand on the boy's shoulder. "Good, then. You an' me, we're friends again. Right?"

"Yessir."

"No more cryin' now, hear?"

"I ain't gonna cry no more, but I ain't ever gonna forget my promise neither."

"Good. Where's your pa?"

Wilbert mumbled something Ben could barely hear. "Speak up, son. I can't hear you. But I guess I already know where your pa is, don't I?"

"Yessir. He's at the Drovers'. He tol' me to wait here an' he'd be along shortly, but he's been gone a powerful long time."

Ben nodded his head. "You go on into the café an' tell Bessie I want you to have a piece of pie with a big scoop of ice cream on it, OK?"

Wilbert's smile was like a blaze of sweet sunshine on a gray and rainy day. He ran off to O'Keefe's.

The Drovers' Inn was an ugly scar on the face of Burnt Rock's Main Street. Gambling, the sale of alcohol, and the carrying of firearms were legal in Texas. Prostitution, however, was not legal, and Ben had put an end to it the day he'd been sworn in. He patrolled the bar several times a night, always disgusted by the braying, drunken laughter and the curses that flowed out the batwing doors and into the street like raw sewage. The majority of those who spent time in Ben's cells were arrested in or near the Drovers' Inn, and two men, made bold and stupid by liquor, had challenged Ben with weapons. One of them was dead and buried in an unmarked tomb outside of town in the area of the cemetery reserved for the poor and the unknown. The other was serving time for bank robbery in Yuma, Arizona.

Ben stepped through the batwings and stood still for a moment, allowing his eyes to adjust to the dim light and the heavy cloud of tobacco smoke. Talking and laughing stopped as all eyes swung toward him. The stench of stale beer, sweat, vomit, and long-unwashed men struck Ben like a blow, but he kept his face neutral. He walked the length of the bar to its end, where a buffalo of a man dressed in denim pants and a filthy shirt sat slouched over his glass of amber liquid. A long-barreled army Colt hung in a holster on the man's hip.

Ben tugged the buffalo's pistol from its holster and dropped it to the damp sawdust covering the floor, then buried his right fist deep into the big man's gut. The second punch flattened an already misshapen nose that had been broken many times before.

Ben held Wilbert's pa up by a handful of shirt to keep him from collapsing on the floor. "If you ever come into my town again with a weapon cocked, I'll break it over your head," he snarled. "Is that real clear?" He released

66

his grip, and the buffalo dropped to the floor. Ben walked the length of the bar again and then went through the batwings to the street. Once out, he stopped and took a huge draught of clean, fresh Texas air.

Most of the welcoming committee had gone back to their homes or their jobs by the time Ben returned to the café. Rev Warner sat at a table with Lee and Missy, and Bessie and Mike hustled about cleaning and re-arranging tables for dinner. Ben pulled up a chair.

"Everything OK, Ben?" Lee asked.

"Yeah. It is now. That fool Buck Starrett carried a rifle under his wagon seat, cocked and ready to fire. His boy started messin' with it and dropped it and it went off."

He rested his right hand on the table but quickly withdrew it and put it in his lap. His knuckles were freshly abraded and there was blood on them. But the move was too late—he knew Lee had seen them.

"That shot gave me a start," Warner said. "I almost fell over, I was so scared. I kind of lost my balance and had to grab a table to keep from falling and making a fool of myself." He smiled. "It wouldn't make the best impression—the new preacher sprawled out on the floor."

Ben's eyes flicked to the preacher's, held them for a moment, and then looked away.

"You couldn't have made a better impression than you did, Rev," Missy gushed. "All of us know we made the right choice."

The preacher smiled at Missy. "I thank you for your kind words," he said. Then he turned his attention to Ben. "Your job is a dangerous one, Marshall Flood. I'll keep you in my prayers."

67

Ben nodded. "Thanks, Rev—and it's Ben from now on, OK? We don't hold with a whole lot of, uhh . . ."

"Rigid convention?" Rev Warner offered.

Ben's eyes tightened for a moment and then relaxed. "Yeah," he said. "Rigid convention."

Lee smiled at Ben. "I've invited Rev and Missy out for dinner on Monday. Carlos and Maria will be there too. Can you make it?"

"I don't see why not," Ben said. "I'll look forward to it—'specially if you're makin' chicken an' dumplings."

"That's the menu," Lee said. "And I'll make an extra bowl of mashed potatoes, just the way you like them."

"Great. A man couldn't ask for more'n that." He shifted his attention to the preacher. "You don't have a horse, Rev. If you like, I'll introduce you to Howard over at the stable. He's got a good string in his barn just now—an' he'll give you a fair price. Maybe you want to take a look at what he has."

"That's already been taken care of, thanks to Lee," Warner said. "I'll soon be the owner of a good horse and a saddle and bridle. I'll ride out with Missy in her surrey on Monday and ride back on my own mount. But I appreciate the offer."

Ben's eyes moved to Lee, questioning.

She answered him. "I'm going to give Rev one of my wrangler remounts. I'm feeding more of them than I have any use for, particularly with winter coming up. There's a nice gray gelding with an easy temperament. The boys call him Chowder. Know the one I mean?"

Ben nodded. "Sure. Pete used him a bit—said he was a good horse. Matter of fact, Pete hauled a foundered mare outta a mud hole with Chowder, as I recall."

"Right—that's the horse."

"Your boys will miss him," Ben said, and then wished he hadn't.

"One thing I have is plenty of horses," Lee said quickly. "And, like I said, with the price of feed going up all the time, I'm feeding too many of them that don't do a lick of work."

Ben suddenly felt uncomfortable. He stood. "Well, I've got things that need doin'. Lee—Missy—Rev—I'll see you on Monday. And I'll warn you all now—don't get between me and that chicken an' dumplings."

Monday didn't work out at all for Ben Flood.

As he was taking up the cinch on Snorty's saddle in the enclosure behind his office, gunfire, shouts, and the chilling sound of shattering glass erupted in the air. All of this was followed by the pounding of hooves on Main Street. Ben secured the cinch, vaulted onto Snorty's back, and raced him through the open gate of the enclosure. As he charged toward the mouth of the alley between his office and the next building, two cowboys hurtled past at a gallop, both swinging wide loops over their heads.

When Ben cranked Snorty into a skidding left turn to pursue the cowhands, he saw the problem: The street was choked from sidewalk to sidewalk with angry longhorns. The eight or ten head the two wranglers were chasing had a good head start and were running hard. Ben swung Snorty back toward the center of town and groaned.

Several cattle had just entered Scott's Mercantile—without opening the door. A steer stood on the sidewalk, shaking his massive head, trying to dislodge a lady's skirt and petticoats from the end of his right horn. A woman screamed from somewhere near the bank. Several more cowboys charged past, working a group of cattle toward the railroad depot.

The heavy crack of a shotgun sounded over the bawling of cows, rebel yells, and screams. A bull with a span of almost five feet between the sharp tips of his horns dropped to his side a few feet from the batwings of the Drovers' Inn. Ben slammed his horse down the sidewalk toward the saloon, swerving and dodging the charging beef.

"Put up that shotgun before you kill someone!" Ben bellowed at the shooter standing just inside the saloon. "I hear another shot, an' I'll close this cesspool down for good!"

A cowhand attempted to cut off a steer heading toward the photography studio, but the panicked animal paid no attention to the rider or his finely trained cow horse. Instead, the steer crashed through the door like a highballing locomotive through a drift of snow. An eye-searing burst of magnesium light flashed for the smallest part of a second before a tremendous cacophony of breaking glass and splintered wood filled the air.

Ben didn't carry a lariat on his saddle, but he saw that the wranglers were going to need all the help they could get. He turned back toward Scott's, rode into the store through the smashed doorway, and yelled to the frenzied clerk, "Gimme a good thirty-foot throwin' rope!"

Four hours later, Snorty was dripping sweat and so was Ben. The cowboys from the Circle R—the group who'd brought the herd in and then lost control of them when the boom of an empty boxcar being secured to a locomotive started a stampede—were settled into the Drovers' Inn. For once, Ben paid no attention to the yelling, the horse racing on Main Street, or the fistfights. After cooling Snorty, rubbing him down thoroughly, and rationing feed and fresh water, Ben felt the fatigue hit him like a bludgeon. He rarely splurged the twenty cents for a hot bath at the barber shop, but he did so that night. His hands were raw and tingling from handling his rope, his shoulders and arms were leaden and sore from wrestling with steers, and his legs were bruised and aching from being rammed by cattle.

He sank into the hot water like a ship going down on a calm sea, sighing with pleasure at the heat. The knots in his muscles began to ease almost immediately, and a prolonged dunk of his head under the surface of the huge tub washed the sweat and grit from his face and hair.

"Care for a cigar, Marshall?" the barber asked.

"No thanks, Horace. I 'preciate the offer though."

"Lots of my customers have them a smoke while they're soakin'. I know you don't use no spirits, so I won't offer you none. Tell you what, though—there's still a light on over to O'Keefe's. How'd you fancy a cold sarsaparilla?"

"I can't think of a thing that'd suit me better, Horace," Ben said. "There's some change in my vest over on the chair."

"Your money's no good here tonight, Ben. The bath an' the drink is on me. I seen you workin' them cows with the Circle R boys. You done that an' you kept the town together too—an' don't you think we all don't appreciate it."

"Part of the job, Horace."

The shop was silent after Horace turned the closed sign to face the street and walked to O'Keefe's Café for the marshal's sarsaparilla. Ben soaked in the tub, doing his best to ignore the occasional yells of the cowhands. That he'd missed dinner at Lee's house was the only real regret he had about the day. It had been a long time since he'd worked cattle, but his skills were still there, and he believed he'd shown the cowhands that a lawman can toss a loop and bulldog a steer.

There'll be lots of other dinners with Lee. But that thought soon became a question—a question that snatched away his peace. Would there be other dinners? Was Lee tired of waiting for him to ask her to marry him? Had she already decided that she couldn't share her life with a man who had a good chance of stopping a bullet every day he went to work?

When Horace returned to his shop, Ben was dried off, dressed, and pulling on his boots.

"Marshall—what're ya doin'? If the water cooled some, I'll warm her up right quick. I got a kettle on the stove."

"The bath was great, Horace, an' I thank you for it. But I got things to do at the office." Ben put on his Stetson and walked out of the barber shop, leaving behind Horace clutching a tall glass of sarsaparilla in his hand.

Hoofbeats outside brought Lee from her chair at the table to her kitchen window. "Maybe that's Ben," she said. "Better late than . . . oh, it's just one of the wranglers." She forced a smile as she sat down.

"Ain' much time Ben can call hees own," Carlos said. "Somethin' goin' on in town, Lee. He would no miss your cheeken dinner less he had to."

"When duty calls a lawman, I suppose he has no options," Rev Warner said. "It's a shame he had to miss this wonderful dinner and the conversation we've had."

"Ees true, Rev Warner," Maria said. "Ben—he work too hard."

"He does for sure," Missy added with a vigorous nod of her head.

The after-dinner chatter drifted away from Lee. *Was it a drunk who needed to be put in a cell? A stolen horse? A fistfight in the street? Couldn't this one night he have left the town on its own for a few hours? How will Rev Warner feel about his absence? Isn't welcoming a new preacher, making him feel at home at least as important as—*

Laughter jolted Lee back to her kitchen. She forced a guilty laugh, having no idea what had been said.

"So," Rev Warner concluded, "that was the last time I tried to scare away a polecat by hollering at him. But I'll tell you this: You never saw a congregation leave a church as fast as those folks did—and the minister was one of the first through the door!"

The laughter began again, and again Lee joined in without real feeling. It had been a good visit, but Ben's chair was conspicuously vacant. She picked up her cup and sipped at her tea.

"Do you have your first sermon all planned out, Rev?"

"To some degree," Warner answered. "You see, I'm not much of a public speaker." He held up his hand as Missy began to protest. "Please—hear me out," he continued. "The Lord puts the words in my heart. I simply articulate them. I've found that the Lord knows a whole lot more about spreading his Word than I do."

There was quiet laughter at that comment. Carlos burped surreptitiously behind his hand. Maria nudged him sharply with her elbow.

"More tea, anyone?" Lee asked. "Rev? Missy? Carlos? Maria?"

All declined, easing their chairs back from the table.

73

"No thanks, Lee," Warner said. "But I do thank you for the splendid meal. I'm only sorry Marshall Flood couldn't make it. And I don't know how to even begin thanking you for the horse. I'm truly blessed. Rest assured that Chowder will receive the best of care."

"I'm sure he will, Rev. Thanks for coming. It's been a lovely evening."

Carlos stood and shook hands with the preacher. "*Sí.* And thank you, Lee. Ees time for me an' Maria to head home. The sun, it come up early roun' here."

Maria joined Carlos and Warner as they walked to the door. "*Gracias,* Lee, *mi amiga,*" she said. "As always, your cheeken was *perfecto.*"

Missy hung back in the kitchen as the two men and Maria stepped outside. "Are you all right, honey? You didn't say much tonight."

"I'm fine, Missy. A little tired maybe, after all the excitement." She smiled and grabbed Missy's hands. "Our church has a preacher! Our prayers have been answered."

"Praise God!" Missy exclaimed. Then she lowered her voice to a whisper. "Have you ever seen such manners on a man?"

"He's going to be a good influence on all of us, I think," Lee said as she walked with Missy to the door. After the woman was settled in her surrey, Lee watched as she drove off with Rev, on Chowder, riding beside her. Carlos and Maria's house was already dark. Light from the moon sifted through strands of clouds, softening sharp edges, casting a gentle glow on the Busted Thumb. Lee turned off her lamps in the kitchen, but instead of going to bed, she sat at the table for a long while. *It was a good evening,* she thought. *Rev Warner has an air about him—a gift from the Lord—that will*

74

benefit all of us in his flock. She smiled. *Missy would jump through a flaming hoop for the man already, and Carlos and Maria were charmed as well. Carlos even opened up about how well the horse operation at the Thumb is progressing.*

Yes, it had been a good evening.

Rev Warner's first sermon in his new town and church was a success. He strode about the area behind the newly varnished pulpit, making excellent use of the space afforded to him. His voice was resonant, powerful—almost theatrical—and he used it with practiced skill. His whisper was a peaceful interlude, and when his tone and volume rocked from the barely audible to the righteous thunder of cannons, his congregation fell under not only the spiritual strength of his words but also the seductive flow of his presentation.

Rev Tucker hadn't been much of a public speaker. He relied on the truth of Scripture and his own convictions and faith to offer ideas and counsel to those he addressed. The difference between the styles of the two men was so vast that it was disconcerting to some.

"Reminds me of that stage play we seen in the big city," Will Butterridge commented to his wife, loud enough so that his raspy, eighty-year-old voice could be heard throughout the church. Tessa Butteridge, red-faced, responded just as loudly, "Hush, ya ol' coot." If the new preacher heard the exchange—and it was likely that he had—he gave no sign.

Rev Warner stood at the front doors of the church afterward, shaking hands and accepting praise for his sermon. Missy Joplin dawdled in the church until Rev Warner was alone.

"Don't you take for serious what that ol' fool Will Butteridge said durin' your talk," she said. "He never did have the sense of a bale of hay."

The preacher smiled. "Maybe I was a bit dramatic," he said.

"Don't worry 'bout that. The whole congregation enjoyed your words, Rev. Will, he'd find a problem if Gabriel hisself was up in front tootin' his horn." Missy reached into her beaded handbag and pulled out four gold coins. "Don't you say no to this money," she told him. "There ain't a man in the world who don't have some expenses, preacher or not. You're gonna hafta buy feed an' hay for the horse Lee gave you—an' you'll need shoes and so forth for him."

Rev Warner shook his head. "I surely do appreciate your kindness, Missy. But a widow lady such as you can't have much money to spare. I really can't accept—"

"Pshaw, Rev," Missy said. "My departed husband never laid out a dime that didn't bring in five dollars. I have more money than I'll ever need. It ain't like I'm a sweet young thing, jist startin' my life neither. I want to use what I have to do good."

Rev Warner pocketed the gold eagles and thanked Missy again.

Lee and Ben stood together outside the church. They both smiled as Rev and Missy walked out into the sunshine. Lee pulled her shawl around her shoulders more snugly. The breeze that scurried around the churchyard promised that autumn was pushing summer away.

She greeted Missy with a warm smile and held out her hand to Warner. "How's Chowder treating you, Rev?" she asked.

76

"Great. Seems like I've spent more time on him than I have off for the last couple of days. We're getting to know one another well."

"Chowder's a good mount," Ben said, "but he's a smart horse, and the smart ones are the ones you need to be careful of."

"He's a clever one, that's for sure," the preacher said. "But I haven't had any problems. He's a tad pigheaded at times, but maybe he's just testing me, seeing what I'll put up with and what I won't."

Lee caught Ben's eyes for a second, and then each one looked away. When the conversation changed to matters of the church board, Ben wandered to the hitching rail where the preacher's horse was tied.

Chowder—Ben remembered the gelding's name had come from the washed-out, grayish color of his coat, which matched the hue of prairie chowder, a meatless stew made of whatever a chuck wagon cook had on hand—was the type of horse a man would call "handy." Chowder moved gracefully and carried himself proudly. Ben had seen him work cattle, and the horse had real cow sense. He'd taunt a bull but keep away from the hooking, razor-sharp horns, and he'd cut a calf from its mama as smooth as an eagle arcing lazy figure eights in the sky.

Ben breathed on Chowder's muzzle—into the animal's nostrils—as he stroked his neck. That breath exchange, Ben knew, was like the human custom of shaking hands. Chowder huffed softly back at him, remembering his scent.

There were bits of dried sweat on Chowder's chest, Ben noticed. He stepped to the horse's side, and his eyes stopped at the barrel, just in front of the rear cinch of the double-rigged saddle. There was dried sweat there

77

too, and faint rowel marks. Ben walked to the other side of the horse and ran his fingers over more spur trails. His face reddened and his jaw tightened. None of Lee's men who'd used Chowder ever felt the need to gouge him with spurs.

There was a pair of fancy Mexican silver spurs hanging from straps around the saddle horn. Ben tapped the point of a rowel with his fingertip and grimaced in anger. Not only were the points too long and too sharp, but the rowel barely moved when Ben attempted to spin it—meaning the sharp peaks would grind against the horse's flesh rather than roll easily.

Ben took the spurs from the saddle horn and stood looking down at them in his hand for a long moment. When he returned to Missy, Lee, and Rev Warner, he felt his face redden with anger.

"Rev," he said, "I hope you won't take this wrong, but you don't need these things with Chowder. He isn't used to spurs, and that's probably why he's been acting up a bit. You'll do better with leg pressure and a light touch on the reins."

Lee looked at the pair of spurs in Ben's hand. A quick spark flared in her eyes. "Ben's right. I hope you'll throw the spurs away. Some horses need a little gentle prodding at times during their training, but not with spurs like this. The wranglers call them 'gut-rippers' because they actually hurt the horse."

Rev Warner's face flushed. "I certainly didn't know any of that," he said. "I was talking with an old fellow in front of Scott's, and he told me those spurs were exactly what I needed. I . . . I'll get rid of them right away. I'm really quite sorry—but I erred from ignorance, not from any desire to hurt—"

"We know that, Rev," Lee interrupted. "I'm sure there's been no harm done. But please—come to me or Ben or Carlos with any horse questions. OK?"

"Absolutely. Ben, give me those things. I'll get rid of them right away."

Ben nodded. "Good idea." He handed the spurs to the preacher as if they were a dead snake rather than metal and leather. Then Missy tugged at the preacher's sleeve.

"Come on, Rev," she said. "My pie has been settin' on my windowsill coolin' since before service, an' I can hear it callin' out to ya."

Warner cupped his ear, grinning. "I believe I can hear it, Missy. Ben, Lee? You'll excuse us?"

Lee and Ben watched as the preacher and Missy walked to her surrey. Lee felt an unease emanating from Ben.

"It was an honest mistake," she said.

"Maybe," he replied. "Here's the thing, though. A man doesn't have to be born on horseback to know those rippers will hurt a horse."

"One of those old coots who sit in front of the mercantile gave Rev bad advice is all. You know how those fellows have an opinion on everything under the sun."

"Sure. But still. . . . No, I guess you're right."

"He's a good man, Ben."

"Sure. I know that." He checked the position of the sun. "Whew—time's gettin' away. I promised Snorty a good rubdown. I'll see you during the week, OK?"

"I hope so. I owe you a chicken dinner with all the trimmings." She hesitated, then added, "Just the two of us, OK? To make up for the dinner you had to miss."

Ben's smile was broad, and the tightness left his face. "I'd like that, Lee."

79

Snorty stood with his eyes half closed, luxuriating in the warmth of the sun tempered by the cool breeze that blew in off the prairie. The stallion perked up his ears when he heard Ben approaching, and snorted his usual wet greeting.

Ben pulled the reins from the loose loop they formed over the hitching rail and swung into the saddle. The toes of his boots found his stirrups as unconsciously as his right hand so often dropped to the handles of his Colt. He pointed Snorty toward town and put the slightest bit of leg pressure against his sides. A one-horse covered cart rattled up behind him.

"Marshall Flood! You! Marshall Flood!" The screeching voice sounded like the angry squeal of a pig. Ben sighed, considered putting Snorty into a gallop, and then made a wide circle back to where Mrs. Loftus Pestle sat, her eyes as dark as a crow, glaring at him as if she'd just caught him with his hand in her purse.

"I want you to *execute* that rooster this time, sir! In fact, I demand that you do so!"

Ben drew rein in front of the old widow. "What happened this time, Mrs. Pestle?" he asked.

"That . . . that . . . creature came right into my house this morning. It's bad enough I have to listen to that horrible voice every morning, but this takes the cake. He came right in through my kitchen window and strutted around like a king. When I went to shoo him out, he *attacked* me, Marshall."

"It's just a rooster, Mrs. Pestle," Ben said as gently as he could, "and folks have every right to keep chickens around their homes. I'll talk to the Shermans again, but you can't expect them to put their ol' rooster on a leash, can you?"

"Don't you dare make fun of me, sir. He came into my home. That's breaking and entering, isn't it? What are you going to do about it?"

"Ma'am—"

"Perhaps if you didn't spend so much time drinking coffee at O'Keefe's and mooning over Miss Morgan, you'd have more time to protect the citizens of this town!"

"Yeah, maybe so," Ben agreed. "Like I said, I'll talk to the Shermans again." He tipped his Stetson and eased Snorty away from the sputtering old woman.

Burnt Rock was quiet, as it almost always was on Sundays. Of course, the Drovers' Inn and its denizens had no more respect for the Sabbath than a scorpion would—the out-of-tune tinkle of the piano reached Ben's ears as he unlocked the back door to his office. He walked past the empty cells and through the door to the front of the building and sat behind his desk. He hadn't replenished the wood in the potbelly stove this morning, so the fire had died. If he wanted coffee, he'd have to start from scratch. It seemed like more trouble than it was worth.

Without much interest, he pushed through the WANTED posters, state notices, and other papers that almost covered the top of his desk. He rolled his chair back and toed open the lower drawer to rest his feet on. A cheery little tinkling sounded as something in the drawer tapped against some glass. Curious, he leaned forward and looked into the drawer. A pint bottle and a pair of old handcuffs. He shook the drawer slightly, and the tinkling repeated. He picked up the bottle.

The label read "Blended True Rye Whiskey," and he remembered taking it from the pocket of a drunken cowhand before he locked the man in a cell. Usually he poured the contents of the bottles of those he arrested into the dirt behind his office. He remembered the day of that particular arrest—he'd been frantically busy and must have dropped the whiskey into his drawer, intending to dump it later. He held the pint in his hand.

He'd had a problem with booze at one time. He hadn't touched a drink in years and hadn't found it difficult to leave the alcohol behind. But for reasons he couldn't quite comprehend, today he wanted a drink.

Lee flashed in his mind, and he saw her smiling at Rev Warner.

A cloud shifted away from the sun, and a beam pierced the office window and turned the liquid in Ben's hand into the amber color of clover honey. The cowboy hadn't had time to open the bottle; the cork was sealed and the line of wax around it was unbroken.

It's been a long time since I had a taste of whiskey. Ben fingered the cork, feeling the dryness of its surface, the cool smoothness of the wax around its base. He stood and tucked the bottle into his back pocket, making sure the neck didn't protrude in plain sight. Outside in the enclosure behind his office, he saddled Snorty mechanically, giving no conscious thought to what he was doing.

A little ride to give myself time to think. Maybe exactly what I need is a little red-eye. It'll calm me down a bit, let me have some room in my head to figure out what's happening with Lee an' me an' my life. Maybe I'll see what it is about the preacher that makes me wonder about him . . .

He put the pint of whiskey in his saddlebag before he mounted. After riding up the alley next to his office, he turned in the opposite direction from the church. He continued on at a lazy walk to where the houses of the first residents of Burnt Rock stood, alongside the new ones being built. He smiled and tipped his hat to a lady who was watering the flower box that lined her front porch. Matt Sherman was in his rocker on the front porch, sipping from a mug and leafing through a Sears, Roebuck and Co. catalog. Ben could hear Matt's wife playing the piano inside. He reined Snorty to a stop.

"That vicious rooster of yours tore into Widow Pestle today, Matt," Ben said. "About wrecked her house too."

"So I heard," Matt said, grinning. "Thing is, I was lookin' out the kitchen window an' I seen Mrs. Pestle whalin' on my poor bird with a broom, screamin' and swingin' at him like he was Satan hisself. She run him right under my porch, an' he didn't come out for over an hour."

"That's about what I figured. Maybe you can send your missus over to calm the widow down a bit?"

"Sure. Fact is, Millie's bakin' up a cake right now for Mrs. Pestle. That'll keep her till the next time."

Ben nodded. "I'd hate to have to try to bring that rooster in, Matt. From what I hear, he's fast an' dangerous. I'm right scared of him, is the truth of the matter."

"I don't blame you. Only thing I can tell you is get rid of that Colt and carry a broom with you, instead."

"I'll think on that," Ben said, laughing with his friend. He put Snorty into an easy lope and rode beyond the houses and into the prairie. When he was four or five miles outside of town, he stopped and looked around at the seemingly endless panorama of buffalo grass. A rise behind him blocked his view of the town he'd just left. He turned in his saddle and took the pint from his saddlebag. He twisted the cork to break the seal and then pulled it free. The harsh scent of whiskey reached him immediately.

A couple of swallows ain't goin' to hurt nothin'. Thing is, I could really use a drink. The image of the late Rev

Tucker flooded his mind. *"The worst possible time to take a drink is when you think you need one or deserve one,"* Rev had said. *"But why not leave it alone completely, Ben? I know you can do this if you make a single promise to me and to yourself: that you'll always say a prayer for direction before you take a drink. Will you promise that?"*

Ben bowed his head. His lips moved silently.

A smile stretched across his face as he opened his eyes. He hurled the bottle up and away, and then his hand closed over the bone grips of his Colt. The pint took a strange flip, and his first shot missed it. His second took it square on, sending out dripping shrapnel that glinted in the sunlight. His third round shattered the largest piece his eyes could find. He fired his last three bullets at the remains that littered the ground.

On the ride back to Burnt Rock, he thought about Lee.

6

Slick danced at the end of the lead line, nostrils flared, coat gleaming in the morning sun, eyes crackling with mischief. Lee tugged him closer with the lead and stroked his neck. "Feeling your oats, my friend?" she murmured. "Does this weather make you want to run?"

"Lee, look here," Carlos called from the small horse trough in front of the main barn. "Ees the first—how do you say?—hide of ice thees year."

"Hide?" Lee asked.

"*Sí.*" He tugged at the flesh on the back of his hand. "Hide."

Lee bit back a chuckle. "I think you mean skin, Carlos."

Carlos thought for a moment. "Ees the same thing, no?" He walked closer to Lee. "An' Maria, she saw a woolly bear in the garden, an' hees band wass *muy* wide—the tan part. Means early winter an' hard winter."

"I guess I don't trust caterpillars much," Lee said with a smile. "But the frost last night was a heavy one."

"Wass a keeling frost. No more garden."

"What a summer, though." Lee pointed at three massive, rounded tarps staked in the pasture next to the barn. "Three cuttings of hay, Carlos—and each of them good, rich cuttings."

He motioned toward the stored hay. "I don' like to keep it under the tarps much, but the barn weel no hold another bale. You know, the rain, she come thees summer like the farmers, they talk to God an' he send it when they want it."

"Maybe that's exactly why we had the rain we did." She looked over at the mounds. "We'll use the outside hay first. Make sure you tell the men to check for rot and powder when they feed it to the horses."

"*Sí.* I already done that." He patted Slick on the rump. "Like touchin' a rock," he observed. "Look in hees eyes, Lee—thees boy wants to play today. Say, you hear that the boy with the ceegarette—Henry—that he ees meesing?"

"Henry? No. What do you mean 'missing'?"

"No one seen heem for two, three days. Bessie tol' me yesterday when I take the wagon to have the wheel feex. I theenk he jus' move on, ees all. Boys like heem, they drift, go here, go there. I talk to heem a month ago an' offer heem feefty cents to help me load the sacks of grain at the mill. He tell me it no ees worth hees time. A boy like that, Lee, I dunno. Don' seem to be much good."

Lee placed her saddle blanket on Slick. He reached around, grabbed it between his teeth, and shook it like a child playing with a flag.

"He gonna give you a ride today," Carlos observed.

Lee smiled, tugged the saddle blanket free from Slick's mouth, and replaced it on his back. A sharp "Hey you!" stopped him from snatching it again.

"I don't know Henry," Lee said, hefting her saddle from the hitching rail and positioning it on Slick. "I've seen him just about every time I've been in town, but I haven't spoken a word with him since I gave him the ride and he got smart with me. Rev told me he's working with the boy, talking with him about the Lord. He said if we knew of Henry's early life, we'd understand him better."

"Laziness ees no hard to understand. He do nothin' in town but hang around, no?"

"Rev said he works cleaning up Howard's smithy shop and barn for some food and a place to sleep. Howard gave the boy that old mare of his—the gray that foundered a couple years back. If Henry wasn't doing good work, Howard wouldn't have done that."

"Maybe. Maybe not. Cleanin' stalls a couple hours a day ees no real work."

Lee laughed. "Give the kid a chance. He could turn out OK."

"Don' matter now," Carlos said. "He's meesing. We won' see heem no more."

Slick snorted as Lee swung onto his back. "Maybe you're right," she said. She scratched behind Slick's ear. "I'm going to take a look at the fences in the west pasture and see if I can burn some of the friskiness out of this fellow."

Lee held Slick to a lope, taking in the taste of the pristine, chilled air. When she gave her mount his head, the initial burst of speed thrilled her, just as it always did. The wind whipped tears from her eyes almost immediately. She felt as if she were one with her horse, that she *was* Slick, breathing with his massive lungs, reaching out with his tightly muscled forelegs.

When she reined in Slick, her heart was aflame with love. *Thank you,* she prayed. *I don't have the words, Lord, to thank you or praise you enough for the gifts you've given to me.*

Henry was always around—and then he wasn't.

"He ain't never missed a day of work before," Howard the blacksmith told Ben. "I tol' him he could have that ol' swaybacked gray mare of mine, an' the horse is missin' too. Thing is, with the renegades an' outlaws round like what done for poor Rev Tucker months back, I'm a little worried 'bout Henry."

"I'll look into it," Ben promised.

Two days later Ben had covered countless miles of prairie looking for Henry or tracks or any sign at all of the young man. He had come up empty.

It was Rev Warner who, from behind his pulpit after the Sunday worship service, put the idea of a search party into the minds of his congregation. "My friends," he said, "a lamb from amongst us is missing. I understand that few of us really know Henry, but we all know that he's a child of God. Just as we'd come together with help for any of our friends here in the church, so should we come together in a search for the missing boy."

The preacher scanned the eyes of the congregation. "The prairie is as vast as it is unforgiving. If the horse Henry was riding tripped and fell, the boy could be alive and in pain, waiting for help, perhaps unable to move because of a broken bone or serious wound. Winter is stalking us, my friends. The nights are cold, and the sun during the day has lost its strength."

He raised his voice. "Shall we let that poor, homeless waif await death on the prairie as his strength ebbs and his teeth chatter together throughout each lonely, painful, and desolate night and each endless day?"

There were hushed murmurs from the congregation. Rev Warner stepped away from the pulpit and paced back and forth, clutching his Bible in his right hand, gesturing with his left. "I say to you that we as Christians must seek out and find the child and not only bring him back to Burnt Rock, but bring him to the Lord as well! What I propose is this: Let us put aside our daily duties tomorrow and spend the rest of today equipping ourselves for searching for poor Henry beginning tomorrow at first light—and to continue searching for him until we've found him. We can ride in pairs and keep our partners safe while we scour the prairie for signs of the boy. Each pair should have at least one weapon—a handgun or a rifle—and ride in a designated direction. I'll arrange for a wagon carrying water and hay to set out today, and that wagon can be our meeting point at the close of each day. Surely with all of us seeking the boy, we'll find him before it's too late."

Carlos, sitting next to Ben in the second pew with Lee, Missy, and Maria, leaned closer to the marshall. "That ees *loco,* Ben—putting a bunch of storekeepers who don' know a good track if they see one out on the prairie. An' with guns they don' know how to use. *Loco.*"

"Yeah. It is crazy," Ben whispered back. He stood, his hands resting on the back of the pew in front of him. "Rev?" he called out.

The preacher stopped midsentence and focused on Ben. "Ahh—Marshall Flood," he said. "I'd counted on you for ideas on how best to organize and direct the search. Please, tell us your thoughts."

Ben cleared his throat as the heads of those in the church turned toward him as if awaiting a royal proclamation. His palms felt damp. He wiped them on his denim pants. "It isn't a good plan at all, Reverend," he said. "In fact, it's crazy."

Some of the women gasped, and the mouths of many dropped open in surprise. "Please, hear me out," he continued. "I'm as worried about the boy as anyone else is. I've spent lots of time looking for him and looking for signs that could lead me to him. But . . ."

"But *what*, Marshall?" Rev Warner demanded. "Should we do nothing and let the child die of hunger or exposure?"

Ben felt his face flush. "No. We shouldn't. But we need to face some facts before the town goes out to do something it doesn't know how to do. First, Henry's not a child, as you call him. He drifted here. It's possible he drifted on. We lost Rev Tucker to outlaws—night riders. Do we want to lose more of our people the same way?"

The preacher flinched as if he'd been slapped hard across the face. He lowered his eyes to the floor in front of him and stood motionless.

Sam Turner stood and turned to Ben. "Perhaps you're a bit too quick in your assessment, Marshall. Rev Warner has a point—the more who look for the boy, the better the odds of finding him."

"Ain't like you to spout off like that, Ben," Missy chided. "'Specially to a man of God goin' about God's good works!"

Ben's face tightened. He hesitated, choosing his words carefully. "I meant no disrespect to Rev Warner. But it ain't—*isn't*—safe out there for people who're used to life in town. Look—suppose I deputize Carlos an we pick a few men an' do the search? I'm talkin' about men who can read signs, who can ride fifteen hours a day, who can handle any trouble that comes their way."

The preacher looked up and met Ben's eyes just as Lee spoke from where she sat next to Missy. "You might not be giving fair value to the skills of the folks in Burnt Rock, Ben. All of us on the frontier have to be smart and tough to survive, whether we work in stores or as ranch hands." Her voice was defensive—and that hurt Ben more than her words did.

"I didn't mean to belittle anyone," he protested. "My point is—"

"Please allow me to make my point, Marshall," the preacher interrupted. "You've had your say. Here's mine: The law I follow is that of God, not that of man. God tells us through Scripture that it's our duty as his children to help others who need our aid and assistance. That's what I'm going to do, and that's what those who follow me are going to do." He turned away from the congregation to walk slowly to his place at the pulpit. "Please pray with me for success in our search," he said.

Ben remained standing for a moment. Then he sat and brought his hands together in his lap. The moment the prayer was completed, he and Carlos left the church.

"It ees no right, Ben," Carlos muttered as they walked to the rail where their horses were tied. "These people, they don' know what's out there. Ees better the boy should stay los' than we lose some more people."

"I'm not even sure that Henry is lost, Carlos. The whole thing doesn't feel right. The kid came here from wherever—he never told anyone—an' he hung around here all this time, an' now he's gone. I think he either just decided to up and leave Burnt Rock, or . . ."

"Or what, Ben?"

91

"I don't know. I just don't know." He shook his head, trying to dismiss a bad thought. "All these folks out there ridin' around in circles, ready to put a bullet in any stranger they see, thinkin' he's a renegade—it's nothin' but trouble. Once they're out of sight of the town, those people won't know where they are. Sure as the sun in the morning, someone's gonna get lost or hurt—or worse."

Carlos untied his reins. "You wanna get some things together now an' ride out, or wait till morning?"

"Well, I spent a couple of days out there and didn't find a thing. If the boy is gone, he's gone—and if he's dead, he's dead. I can't spend any more time worrying about him, with half my town playing Texas Ranger. Let's wait until tomorrow, give Rev Warner and his people some lead time, and then ride herd on 'em, keep 'em from gettin' lost an' from shootin' each other. I'd bet a dollar against an onion that they'll all have had enough of the prairie in a day or so."

"Can you no order them not to do thees?"

"Not legally. There's nothin' against the law about gathering a search party." Ben shook his head sadly. "Even if there was, I got a feeling they wouldn't listen to me. Look, your oath as deputy is still good from the last time, far as I know. I'll give you the badge tomorrow."

"Ees good. I'll ride back to the Busted Thumb and put one of my men in charge and look things over. I have a mare who ees about ready to foal, but she's a good ol' gal an' she's had three young ones already without no problem. I'll ride back early tomorrow, no?"

"Thanks, Carlos. I 'preciate the help."

Carlos didn't mount up. "One thing. Did you scout the foothills when you were looking for Henry? If you din't find heem on the prairie, ees 'bout the only place he could be, no?"

"I looked for tracks, but I didn't ride on in. You're right, though. Maybe I should head there while you ride herd on the searchers."

Carlos nodded. Still, he didn't step into a stirrup. "Ben, uhh . . . the preacher and Lee—"

Whatever Carlos was about to say was cut off by Lee's voice from the front of the church. "Ben, hold on. I want to talk with you," she said, holding up her hand. Carlos swung into his saddle, waved, and jigged his horse into a slow lope as Lee hustled across the yard to where Ben stood next to Snorty.

Ben could tell from the sharpness of her eyes that she was angry. And the tone of her voice only reinforced that fact.

"Just what did you hope to gain by taunting Rev Warner like you did in there?" she demanded.

"Taunting? Listen here—the whole idea is stupid. Those people—"

"I don't believe that trying to find a lost child is at all stupid. Do you?"

"Yeah, I do, Lee. You might just as well send a bunch of chickens out looking for a fox. Someone's gonna get hurt, you mark my words. An' that'll happen because a preacher who's spent his whole life in cities decided he's Moses leading God's people."

"That's not fair!"

"Think about it, Lee. Olaf Schermerrer out there with a pistol or a rifle? He can't see beyond his elbow, an' you want him to search for somebody? Dwight Parnell hasn't spent five minutes on a horse's back in the last ten years! Basil Tempa? He hasn't been outta his store since he built the place. C'mon, this whole deal doesn't make any sense."

"We have a good plan. We'll stay as close together as we can. We even decided on some signals to call for help."

"Signals?" Ben tried to keep his voice level, but even in his own ears, it sounded angry.

"Yes, signals. Gunshots. If anybody is in trouble, all he has to do is fire twice and the rest of us will ride toward the sound and take care of whatever the problem is."

Ben shook his head. "It won't work. There are so many hollows an' echos out there that the shots will sound like they came from a dozen different directions."

"Well, Duncan said that—"

"Oh, it's 'Duncan' now?"

"We're friends, Ben. Why do you have to be like this?" Lee's voice was level, but a blush crept into her cheeks.

"I suppose you're going to be part of this search party," Ben said, trying to ignore the blush.

"Yes. I ride better than any man in town, and my Slick is the best horse."

Ben had to chew on the inside of his cheek to keep from responding to that.

"And I can handle a pistol and a rifle. Plus, I know the area as well as you do. I need to be part of the search."

"You're . . . never mind. Forget it." He mounted Snorty and rode away.

Lee stared at the marshall's back as he rode off toward town. All around her, enthusiastic churchgoers climbed into their wagons and mounted their horses, eager to gather supplies together for the morning. There was a strangely festive air about the group, as if they were setting forth on a picnic.

Lee shivered slightly as the breeze from the prairie touched her. Her eyes flicked to the sky and then were held there by the slowly twisting shapes of the high clouds to the north. She shivered again. The sky looked cold.

The preacher's voice pushed into her thoughts. He stood just outside the church, Bible still in hand, calling to her, a concerned look on his face. Even from a distance, Lee could see the warmth in the man's eyes.

"Lee, is something wrong?" His voice was quiet, but she heard his words clearly.

She looked around herself, disoriented for a moment. All the people who'd been scurrying about a few moments ago were gone. She and Rev Warner were alone in the churchyard.

"Is there something I can do to help?" the preacher asked, now standing in front of her. He put his hand on her shoulder so gently that an image of a summer butterfly landing there flickered briefly in her mind. She looked into his eyes and suddenly felt dizzy, as if she might fall.

"Lee?"

She looked down and took a deep breath. Even then, the masculine scents of crisp, clean clothes, shaving talc, and well-polished leather held her almost paralyzed. She forced herself to take the couple of steps that brought her to the hitching rail. Leaning against it, she could feel her knees trembling under her layers of petticoats.

"I'm all right," she said and then forced a smile that she was sure looked more like a grimace. Slick was tied to the hitching rail at the rear of the church, where she'd put him after arriving early to have coffee with Rev Warner before the service. She didn't want to walk over there just now—she wasn't sure her legs would carry her.

"It's silly. I just got a bit dizzy. I'm fine now."

"Trouble with Marshall Flood?" the preacher asked. "About finding poor Henry? Ben's face was red when he left you."

"Not really. It's just that everything's so . . . muddled, I guess. Ben says it's insane for a bunch of city folks to be out there with guns, and that we'll never find the boy anyway. You heard him in church—how he reacted to your idea."

"I'm not quite sure if Ben was reacting to my idea or to me as a person," Duncan said. "I'm not sure of that at all."

Lee sidestepped his comment. "He mentioned some of the men who wouldn't be much use in a search party, and he was right. He's afraid we'll end up shooting at one another."

Duncan was silent for a long moment. When he spoke, his words shocked her. "Do you doubt God? Do you doubt his power?" His voice was level and subdued, but somehow it struck Lee like a riding quirt.

"No! Of course not! Why would you ask that?"

"Do you find it difficult to believe that God speaks to certain of his servants, giving them instructions in things that pertain to their own good and the good of others?"

"No, I don't . . . I mean, I know God speaks to us and that—"

"Well, that's what has happened here, Lee. God spoke to me last night and put this plan to find the child in my mind. I won't—regardless of what Ben Flood or you or anyone else says or believes—go against the word of God. And perhaps it would be good for you and for your relationship with the Lord if you'd spend less time with a man whose life is so inextricably wound through with violence."

"That's not fair! Ben is—"

"The man refuses to help save the life of an innocent child! How can you justify that?" Suddenly, the cold flame in the preacher's eyes went out like a matchstick dashed in water. His shoulders drooped a bit. "I'm sorry, Lee. I . . . I'm sorry," he said and walked hastily toward the church.

The churchyard was quiet—almost desolate—as Lee walked to where Slick was tied. The wind sloughed quietly from the vastness of the prairie beyond the church. The building seemed an imposter, too new and fresh in contrast with the endless buffalo grass swaying and reaching toward the horizon. Lee looked up at the sky again and then set her cinches and mounted.

Slick wanted to run, but he picked up on Lee's confused and somber mood and quieted immediately. He took his cue for a slow lope without argument and began covering the miles to the Busted Thumb Horse Farm.

Lee noticed that the clouds to the north had become more active, seemingly climbing up and over one another and then merging to form a front of pewter-colored cotton. And she couldn't help but notice the sharp drop in temperature carried by the now-punishing wind.

She reined Slick to a stop and looked around, turning in her saddle. The clouds were still building, but there was no scent of rain in the wind. Slick danced under her, feeling the sting in the weather. Lee, realizing her mount's unease, scratched his neck and spoke to him, almost as a mother would speak to a frightened child. The wind swept her words away, but the tone of her voice reassured Slick. When she resumed the lope after tugging her collar a bit more closely around her throat, both horse and rider were glad to be back in motion, heading for the Thumb.

The next morning Carlos and Ben stood next to their saddled horses in the enclosure behind Ben's office, each holding a mug of hot coffee in gloved hands. The sun was making a feeble, halfhearted attempt to rise above the eastern horizon, its light giving little definition to the town.

"This no good, Ben. The storm of '63, she started like thees. Wass early in the winter, jus' like now. Whole herds, they died where they stood, no? I see them. I never forget."

Chewing on his lower lip, Ben stared out into the murky light, seeing next to nothing where he should have seen the backs of the buildings along Main Street. "We gotta talk them out of it. It'll be suicide for them to ride out on their wild goose chase if this develops into a storm."

"The preacher will ride, Ben. I know thees. He isn't a man who lets anything stop heem."

"He's a fool, then," Ben snapped. "No one but a fool would risk the lives of a bunch of . . ." He dropped the sentence and sighed, then took a brass badge from his coat pocket and handed it to Carlos. "Better pin this on. Let's go over to the church and see if we can talk some sense into Warner. But look—if they do go out, we're going to have to break up. I want you to ride herd on the townspeople as close as you can. Like we talked about yesterday, I'm going to head out to the foothills. That's the only place where Henry could still be alive if he did get in some trouble. If he's out on the prairie somewhere, he's dead."

Carlos snorted. "*Sí*. But we don' even know that he's not long gone—jus' rode on without no trouble at all. He could be settin' in front of a fire with hees boots off in a cantina somewheres while we ride aroun' in the col' an' wind looking for heem."

Ben nodded. "Could be. I don't know, though—I have a strange feelin' about this whole thing with the kid leavin' Burnt Rock like he did." Ben stepped into his stirrup. "Let's move, Carlos."

There were a dozen or more men clustered around the front of the church. Near them stood four farm wagons, two covered with tarps on frames to provide shelter and two open. Rev Warner stood in front of the closed church doors. Beside the preacher stood Jack Sowderly, an elderly farmer.

"One thing I know is the weather," Sowderly shouted to the group. "I seen a flock more prairie storms an nor'easters than anybody round here. Ever time there was this kinda yallowish haze to the clouds. Every doggone time! I don' see that now, cause it ain't there." He looked at the gathering, his face flushed as if in anger. "Any of you folks see anythin' yaller 'bout the sky? Sure, it's cold. But there ain't gonna be no storm. An' I'll tell you somethin' else. We ain't near as cold as that poor boy is, settin' there waitin' on us to bring him home!"

Eyes darted to the gray mass overhead and then back to the old man. "Let's get going!" one of the men called. "Jack's right! That boy is cold!"

Ben and Carlos looped their reins over a hitching rail and walked toward the group. Ben saw Slick standing, ground tied, in the shelter of the side of the church, and a hot surge of anger ran through him. He swallowed hard and kept walking.

The men were indistinguishable from one another, standing close together, as if drawing heat from their comrades. All were dressed in long range coats, and their hats were secured to their heads by scarves tied under their chins. They wore farm boots for the most part, although a few were in high riding boots. Their hands were protected by heavy gloves. Several wore gun belts around their waists, and one fellow held a double-barreled shotgun, muzzle pointing down, at his side. Lee's back was to Ben, but he identified her by the cascade of ebony hair that fell down her back.

Ben strode past the cluster of people and stood directly in front of the preacher, facing him. "I ain't gonna let this happen, Rev. Sending folks out into that mess out there is insane. Suppose this weather does swing to a storm? A nor'easter can last for days, an' there ain't anyone here who could survive if he got lost in one."

"Please, Marshall, we heard your views yesterday. This is no longer your concern—it's a matter of good Christians doing as they must, as they've been ordered by God," Warner said, loudly enough for all to hear. Then he continued, "My people, pray with me . . ."

Ben turned to face the group, his eyes seeking, finding, and holding for a moment with those of the individual townspeople. "Carlos and I will ride out right now, and I'll give you my word that we'll either come back with Henry or we'll have done the most thorough search for him any men could do. There's no reason for you to put your lives in danger. You have wives, families, businesses—think of them. This is my job. Let me and my deputy do it without worryin' every second that our friends are riskin' their lives on a fool's mission."

A hand gripped Ben's shoulder from behind. Ben turned and saw the preacher standing there. The preacher removed his hand. "You do your work, Marshall. Let us do ours."

Ben's right hand clenched into a fist. Warner stepped back.

Ben took a deep breath, broke eye contact, and walked stiffly to where Carlos stood. "They're gonna do it," he said quietly to his friend. "Ain't no reasonin' with them. That old goat Jack Sowderly's got them convinced the sky is clear an' the summer sun's out."

"I'll watch them close as I can," Carlos said. "'Least try to keep 'em from shootin' each other."

"Good." Ben sighed. "I'll go ahead, then. If I don't find anything in two days, I'll be back an' join up with you, if they're still searching."

Turning from Carlos, he walked to Lee and stood facing her. "I'm scared, Lee," he said quietly. "I've got to ask you once more, please don't—"

"I'm sorry, Ben. This is something I believe I have to do. I've thought about it and prayed over it, and I have to go." Her words began to tumble out faster, and her voice trembled slightly. "This isn't about you or Rev Warner or anyone else other than a lost boy. We'll find Henry. I know it in my heart."

Their eyes held for a moment. "Be careful," Ben said. He began to lift his gloved right hand to her face, but he held it back. "Be careful," he repeated.

"You too, Ben. You be careful too."

The cold didn't really settle into Ben's bones until he'd been riding toward the foothills for over three hours. It was then that the storm began in earnest. The wind snarled, driving before it glass-hard bits of ice that stung human flesh and horsehide alike. It seemed that nature in its fury could no longer direct or control the wind—

101

it howled from all directions, whirling the ice pellets now mixed with snow into an impenetrable maelstrom.

In a matter of twenty minutes, the footing was treacherous. The ice and drizzle that had preceded the snow now joined with it to create a glaze that even steel horseshoes had difficulty finding purchase on. Ben held his horse to what the Indians called a crawling lope—barely quicker than an extended walk. The gait was strange to Snorty, and he labored at it, arguing with Ben for more rein.

Now they can't *turn back. If only they haven't spread out too far. If only Carlos is able to get them together before their horses panic or they lose all their bearings. If only . . .*

When Ben stopped to dismount and walk for a bit on feet that felt like they were carved from stone, he pulled off his right glove with his teeth and drew his Colt. The arctic coldness of the metal surprised his fingers and palm, sending a message of heat—of having touched a white-hot stove—to his brain.

He unbuttoned the top few buttons of his range coat and thrust the pistol into the holster he had sewn to the fleece lining, just under his left arm. Even through his shirt and his long underwear, the chill of the weapon struck him like a bucket of ice water. He had no choice but to suffer the shivers. The lubrication that allowed the cylinder to turn freely and to function as it should had turned to glue in the bitter cold, and the .45 would be as useless as a chunk of coal if he needed it in a hurry.

Ben cleared the crystalline beard from around Snorty's mouth and stroked the horse's muzzle and neck. Snorty made it very clear that he didn't like this crazy ride at all; he blew through his nostrils and tamped the snow in front of him with angry hooves. Ben checked the cinch and climbed into his saddle, easing his horse into that same grindingly slow pace.

There was no trail to follow, no signs to be noticed and analyzed. He rode in a miasma of shades of gray, pushing a good horse over unsure ground, risking the animal's legs and perhaps his life. Each time one of Snorty's hooves failed to find traction and skidded under him, Ben tensed and his hands shot to the saddle horn to launch himself free if his horse went down. Ben rode by instinct only; there were no landmarks, no familiar swales or outcroppings to guide him. The long minutes turned into hours as he rode, body numb, eyes squinting to protect them from the snow beating into his face.

The buffalo jerky in the deep pocket of his coat had turned to granite, but he shoved a few sticks of it into his mouth to let his saliva soften and warm it. As he worked on the jerky, his mind wandered amid the furor around him.

Lee's falling in love with Rev Warner. The thought— one he'd been avoiding—struck him like the slug from a Sharp's rifle. *He has words I don't know, and he knows things I don't know.*

A break in the wind allowed Ben a moment of less-obscured vision. The mounds of the foothills—white now rather than the green and brown of summer— appeared far ahead. And a thought every bit as cold and cruel as the storm surfaced in his mind.

Maybe I should bow out and let Lee find the life she needs.

He shook his head, chased away the thought, and replaced it with another. *There's somethin' not quite right about Duncan Warner. Somethin' that bothers me a lot. I'm just not sure what it is.*

7

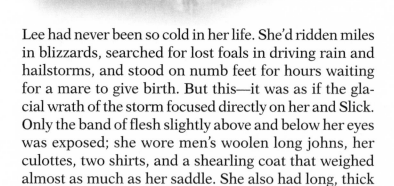

Lee had never been so cold in her life. She'd ridden miles in blizzards, searched for lost foals in driving rain and hailstorms, and stood on numb feet for hours waiting for a mare to give birth. But this—it was as if the glacial wrath of the storm focused directly on her and Slick. Only the band of flesh slightly above and below her eyes was exposed; she wore men's woolen long johns, her culottes, two shirts, and a shearling coat that weighed almost as much as her saddle. She also had long, thick scarves wrapped around her neck and face.

An old Stetson was pushed onto her head, its brim tugged down alongside and tied in place with a length of baling twine. On her hands she wore mulehide gloves lined with jackrabbit fur, but she hadn't been able to feel her fingers in three hours. Inside all of the layers of clothing, her body trembled like that of a person suffering from ague. Tears froze as they were forced from her eyes by the wind, and her lashes were rimmed with crystal ice.

Slick's muzzle was frosted with ice too, and strands of mucus had frozen beneath his nostrils, looking like small stalactites hanging from his jaw. He plodded ahead, unsure of his footing, his muscles tense, transmitting his nervousness to his rider.

The process of a hot bath ran through Lee's mind: the fire licking hungrily at the bottom of the big pot, the boiling water pouring into the deep metal tub, the steam rising in a cloud.

Rev Warner suddenly appeared beside her on Chowder. He eased his horse close to Slick and leaned from his saddle to speak into her ear, over the howl of the wind.

"I'm going to swing off toward the foothills," he said. "I have a feeling that's where he is." He closed his gloved hand over one of Lee's, but she barely felt his grasp. He leaned closer. "Are you all right?"

Lee forced a smile that felt like it tore the flesh of her face. "I'm fine. Don't go too far out alone, Duncan."

He nodded. "There's hot coffee on the wagon. Howard brought a little firebox filled with pea coal like they use on chuck wagons. It'll be a godsend. You look like you could use some." He looked away from her a moment, then looked back. "This snow'll end soon, Lee. I feel like I'm getting close to Henry—it's almost like I can hear him calling to me."

Lee watched as he swung Chowder away. In a brief moment he was gone, now invisible within the storm. In her mind, she saw him at the pulpit in the church, Bible in hand, his voice mellifluous and deep like the faraway rumble of a train. She heard the preacher's words too, and they were filled with promise and hope and kindness. *He's such a believer, so devoted to the Lord.*

A rear hoof slid sideways, and Slick threw his weight against the skid, jolting Lee from her thoughts. She patted the horse's neck reassuringly. In a moment, Ben took over Duncan's place in her mind. Ben was as different from the preacher as any man could be, but in some ways, the men were very similar. Ben was caring too. And both men were loners. Ben and Carlos were friends and had great respect for one another. But in the few hours Ben was able to find for himself, he preferred to ride out alone onto the prairie. Duncan, in the five or so months he'd been in Burnt Rock, hadn't really befriended anyone besides Missy and her. She wasn't sure what he did during his off hours, and she'd not asked him.

But Ben is troubled, she thought. Her mind flashed to the Colt he wore. He'd told her that he slept with it under his pillow. She shuddered, this time not from the cold. She heard the creaking of the supply wagon during a lull in the wind and turned Slick toward the sound.

Ben led Snorty into an overhang of sod and rocks behind a stone face that stood alone, guarding the foothills. The water in his canteen, even though he carried it in a deep pocket of his wool-lined duster, was frozen solid. He could easily eat handfuls of snow to quench his thirst, but his horse didn't have that option.

Ben tugged some pieces of root and scrub from around the base of the stone face where the wind had hurried away any snow that attempted to settle. In his saddlebag he had a block of twenty or so lucifers with their heads encased in paraffin to protect them from dampness, and he fetched them with disobedient, numbed fingers. Twenty minutes of kicking through the snow and circling the face yielded less than an armful of dried branches, weeds, and the husks of tumbleweeds.

He arranged the fuel over his canteen, which he'd placed against the dirt and stone where the face met the ground.

The wind continued to plague him; he used most of his lucifers before the fire caught. It was puny fire, selfish with its heat, but it did what Ben needed it to do. When the flames died, he wrapped his gloved hands in his scarf and picked up the canteen. He plucked the charred cork with his teeth and poured the slushy water into his inverted Stetson at his feet and carried it to his horse. Snorty sucked at the liquid greedily, wanting more when the hat was empty. Ben rubbed the animal's muzzle, wiping away the frost from his nostrils and eyes. Then he mounted and urged Snorty away from the meager protection the stone face had offered.

The single shot was unmistakable, but the wind tore the report into shreds of sound that assaulted Ben's ears from every direction. He held his breath, awaiting another shot that didn't come. His mind churned as he tried to sort the first crack of the shot from the echoes and wind-twisted fragments. It had to have come from ahead and to his right, he decided, since he'd flinched back and to the left. He pointed Snorty ahead and asked for a bit more speed. Snorty responded by lurching into a stiff, awkward canter, plowing through hock-high snow in some places and skidding and sliding on places where the snow had been scoured away. Boulders seemed to pop up from the ground and disappear in the frenetic snow as rapidly as they'd come. Ben felt Snorty stumbling up a slope but couldn't see more than a couple of feet around himself and his horse. He reined in beside a massive boulder, and a blessed break in the wind gave him a heartbeat of clear vision. Fifty yards straight ahead was a dark oval in a long wall of white— a cave. The snow and wind came again, but Ben had zeroed in on the lone dark spot. He pushed Snorty toward it.

The fifty yards felt like fifty miles. The wind was intensifying rather than diminishing, and it now was a keen, high-pitched wail that promised to cut through flesh and bone like a lumber mill saw. A gust slammed Snorty and forced him to stumble, and Ben grabbed at his saddle horn to keep his seat. It was no good; Snorty was going down on his side, flailing his hooves as he fell. Ben pushed off, crashed into hard rock on his side, and grunted in pain as the breath whooshed out of him. When he managed to choke some air into his lungs and stand up, he was alone in the other-worldly clutches of the storm. He stood in place, fighting down panic. A quick, barely formed prayer flickered in his mind and then was gone.

He wanted with all his heart and all his being to run. Even though he knew how incredibly stupid that would be, his senses demanded he flee the storm, like a mouse fleeing an attacking blacksnake. In the frigid and unforgiving cold, sweat broke on his forehead; panic flared in him like an August prairie fire. He attempted a few deep breaths to calm himself, but the icy air in the depths of his lungs brought on paroxysms of coughing. He crouched, scooped snow with his hands, and forced it into his mouth. The razorlike burn of the melting snow helped to steady him. His breathing slowed; the moisture on his forehead froze and was whisked off by the wind.

Ben took his best guess on the direction of the cave and took a step. He took another, and then another, slightly longer this time. Then he walked into Snorty's side.

He didn't know who was more surprised. Snorty, reins snapping in the wind, lived up to his name. He snorted loudly and pushed at Ben with his muzzle. Ben wrapped his arms around the horse's neck and clung to him for a long moment. He realized that Snorty's instinct to run from the storm was even stronger and more compelling than his own had been—and yet the horse had stayed, waiting for his master. Ben shook his head in wonderment, hugged Snorty's neck again, and then stepped into a stirrup.

The closer they came to what was only a slightly less gray mass ahead, the more the howling power of the wind was deflected. When they were still ten yards out, shapes began to form: striated, sculpted banks of snow striped with bands of sand and dirt; a long, tall, sheer stone face that stretched back into the storm on both its ends; and a darker blotch that was the cave. Snorty picked up the pace on his own, surging toward the promise of shelter.

The ceiling at the mouth of what Ben now saw was a cavern rather than the smaller, more tightly confined space of a cave, was high enough for him to ride into, away from the pummeling storm. Toward the rear of the cavern, a small fire glowed. He dismounted and led Snorty deeper into the darkness, toward the blue-yellow flames.

A harsh, raspy moan stopped him in place for a moment, his right hand dropping automatically to his hip for his side arm. His clumsy fingers found only frigid air—his Colt was tucked up under his shirt. He bit down on his right glove with his teeth, dragged his hand out of it, and brought out his weapon. It couldn't be a bear or a cougar, he knew—Snorty would've pitched and kicked in fear if he'd picked up either scent.

Ben moved forward slowly, leaving his horse ground tied. When he was closer to the fire, he saw a form next to it and hurried forward, the frozen heels of his boots clattering against the stone floor. Henry was flat on his back, one arm extended, the other wrapped around his chest. The boy moaned again as Ben crouched next to him. The front of Henry's coat was saturated with blood, and a puddle of dark liquid, frozen and shiny like the ice of deep water, extended around the upper part of his body.

Ben opened the boy's coat. The wound was a bad one, and he was bleeding copiously. The bullet had struck him midchest—the rasp of Henry's breathing told Ben a lung may have been nicked or even punctured. When the boy's eyes fluttered open, he didn't seem to see Ben hovering over him. His pupils remained fixed, glinting in the light of the fire.

Ben stood, hauled off his coat, and tore off his shirt, not taking the time to work the buttons free. He ripped off a sleeve, crumpled it into a tight ball, and then tore long strips from the body of the shirt. He placed the cloth ball over the wound, pressed it inward as much as he dared, and then worked three of the ragged strips under the boy and around his chest, tying them securely enough to hold the makeshift compress in place.

Henry cried out in pain as Ben moved him closer to the fire, and for a moment, his eyes found Ben's. "Preacher . . ." the boy whispered. "Get preacher . . ."

"I'll get him, Henry. There's a wagon nearby—we'll take you to Doc. You'll be . . ."

Ben didn't finish the sentence. Henry's eyes had shut, and he was unconscious again, the only signs of life his shallow, hoarse breathing and the slow tapping of the pulse at his throat. The compress was saturated already, and Ben tightened the strips of cloth holding it in place. He made the boy as comfortable as possible, tucking his coat around him, and then ran to where Snorty stood.

He grabbed his rifle from the saddle scabbard and trotted out of the cavern. He worked the lever and fired, waited

to a count of ten, and then fired twice rapidly, the con-
cussive boom of the shots separated by the smallest part
of a second. He waited three minutes and then repeated
the procedure. As he waited for another three minutes to
elapse, he searched for tracks outside the cavern. As he'd
suspected, the keening wind had broomed away any signs
of whoever had shot Henry. After completing four three-
shot cycles, he returned to the wounded boy.

The cavern was well equipped, Ben found. There was
a mound of branches, cut logs, and kindling next to the
fire. A large, flame-blackened kettle rested next to the
embers, and there was a large sack of jerky next to it.
Two dime novels with brilliantly colored covers had been
placed on an army blanket, one opened to the middle,
as if set down by someone whose reading had been interrupted. Ben read the titles: *Buffalo Bill's Duel with Des-
tiny* and *Deadeye Dick Tames the Cherokees*.

He took the kettle out into the storm and packed it
full of snow. In a matter of two minutes, the fire reduced
the snow to water, which Ben placed in front of Snorty.
He was stripping off his tack from the horse when he
heard a shot, a pause, and then two quick reports. He
sprinted to the mouth of the cavern and echoed the shots
he'd heard. When he received an answer, he began firing a shot every minute or so, guiding the other person
to him.

Carlos appeared suddenly, as if he'd stepped out from
behind a white curtain. Ben couldn't help but grin; Carlos looked very much like a snowman, complete with
protruding white belly and an old hat squashed down
on his head. He was leading his horse, which Ben
noticed was favoring its right front hoof.

"Ahh, Ben," Carlos groused, "this *cayuse* ain't got the
sense of a cheeken. I theenk pretty soon I cut heem open

111

an' climb inside heem for the warmth, like soldiers an' buffalo hunters do. Bill Cody, he do this once an' waited out a blizzard, all nice an' warm. Save hees life."

"What happened to your horse?"

"He sleeped on ice, which ain' so bad. But he come up in great fear an' struck at a rock an' split hees hoof. He'll be OK—the hoof, it'll grow out." Carlos looked around, awed by the cathedral-like aura of the cavern. "You made a fire already? Maybe there's coffee, no?"

Ben filled in Carlos on how he'd come to the cave as Carlos pulled the cinches on his saddle and lifted it and the saddle blanket off his horse's back.

"One shot is all you hear?"

"Yeah. Just one. Henry's hit hard—probably has a bad lung."

"Weel he live?"

Ben shook his head. "I dunno. We need to get him back to town, get him to Doc. He's got no chance at all out here."

"We can no ride in thees, Ben."

"Yeah. I know. We need to wait out the storm and we need the wagon. Where are the others? Is Lee all right?"

Carlos ground tied his horse and tugged off his gloves, shaking the snow and ice from them. "I gather them up aroun' the wagon an' told them no one leaves. That preacher, he ride out anyway. Lee, she argue with me. I tol' her me an' Maria ride away from the Busted Thumb for good if she ride into the weather. She knows I speak truth in such times."

"She's OK, then?"

"Mad as the wet hen, no? But OK."

"The others all accounted for?"

"I theenk so."

They walked back to the fire. Carlos crouched beside the boy and felt his forehead. *"Muy caliente,"* he said. He gently lifted away Ben's coat and inspected the wound, sighed, and draped the coat back over Henry. *"Muy mal,"* he said. "But maybe if we can get heem to Doc, he have a chance."

Ben chewed on his lower lip. "We gotta get the wagon here. We can't wait out the storm—he'll never make it."

"The wagon, it ees maybe three or four mile. I take Snorty an' go there. You stay here with the boy."

"I'll make the ride. You stay here. I'll—"

"No. I know the way an' you don'. You want to be like the preacher, ridin' like a crazy man, not knowin' where you are? No, I go."

Ben tore off another piece of his shirt and wet it in the water at the bottom of the kettle. He stretched it across Henry's forehead and let it settle. The boy stirred slightly, coughed, but didn't open his eyes. Blood mixed with saliva trailed down his chin.

Both men saw it. Neither commented. There was nothing to say.

"Hello? Helloooo?" A weak voice reached into the cavern. Ben and Carlos ran to the front, Ben snatching up his rifle on the way. Once outside, he put two shots into the air. There was no response. He fired another pair and waited. There was no answering report, but the voice sounded again.

"Soun' a leetle closer," Carlos said. Ben emptied the 30.30 into the sky, firing at thirty-second intervals. When he stopped to reload, he heard the ringing clatter of steel horseshoes on stone.

"He's riding too fast," Ben said. "He's gonna go down."

The horse and rider didn't go down. In fact, Duncan Warner nearly collided with the two men. The preacher hauled his horse to a stop and dismounted. Chowder's breathing was wet and croupy as he struggled for air.

"Thank God!" Warner exclaimed. Carlos and Ben stood still, their eyes shifting from Chowder to the preacher. Warner took a step back. "Why are you looking at me like that?"

Ben stepped to Chowder's side and peeled off a ten-inch-long line of dried blood. He patted the horse lightly on his rump and moved forward, placing his ear just in front of the stirrup leathers, tight against Chowder's hide. "You might have broken this horse's wind," he said tightly. "There's a lot of crackling in his lung, and it's probably the same thing on the other side. He was sucking too much cold air too fast."

He glared at the preacher with such intensity that Warner took a step back. "Should I have died so my horse could live?"

"There ees no reason for anyone to die. You are alive now, no? But you hurt the horse who carry you to here." Carlos held Warner's eyes for a moment and then turned away. When the preacher began to speak, Ben cut him off.

"There's no time for this. We got a dyin' boy here, an' we need the wagon."

"You found Henry?" Warner's voice raised in excitement. "Thank the Lord! We found him!" His eyes rested on the fire and the figure stretched out next to it. "He's hurt?"

"He's got a gunshot wound in his chest. You know any medicine, Rev?"

"Some. I helped out on the battlefield during the war. I watched the surgeons treat wounds as big as your fist and pull the soldier through. Maybe I learned enough to help the boy."

The preacher hustled to Henry's side, Ben and Carlos on either side of him. After lifting away the coat, he eased his fingers under the blood-soaked compress. He shook his head and withdrew his hand. Then he put his index finger on Henry's pulse point. When he stood to cover the boy, there was a fingerprint of blood on the spot he'd just touched.

"We need to do two things," he said, as if preaching to a congregation. "We must pray, and we must get Henry to Doc's office. The bullet's probably still inside him, and he's bleeding terribly. The slug has to come out and the bleeding must be stopped, and I can't do that."

Henry's eyes jerked open and focused on the preacher. His Adam's apple moved up and down spasmodically as he tried to force sounds from his throat. His right hand trembled on his chest, and beads of sweat trickled from under the cloth on his forehead.

"He asked for you earlier, Rev," Ben said. "Maybe he wanted you to pray over him."

Warner touched Henry's pulse point again, and the boy's right hand began a spastic dance on his chest. "We don't have much time," the preacher said.

"We no got but one good horse, Ben," Carlos said. "Mine can carry no weight, an' Chowder, he can no go out till he rest maybe two, three hours. Snorty knows me. I go, no?"

Ben nodded. "I wish we could ride together an' leave Rev here." He looked toward the front of the cavern. "Doesn't look to be calmin' down any out there." He chewed his lower lip. "You're the one who knows the way, Carlos. You're the logical one to find the wagon an' the folks and bring them back here. There's no other way." After a moment, he added, *"Vaya con Dios."*

After Carlos left, Ben added wood to the fire and helped himself to a few sticks of jerky. When he filled the kettle with snow again, he let Chowder and Carlos's horse drink, then refilled it and soaked the cloth from Henry's forehead with the cool water. When he touched the boy's face, he felt the vehemence of the fever. He cupped a few tablespoons of water in his hand and let it dribble between Henry's parched, colorless lips. Henry, unconscious again, didn't attempt to swallow. The water seeped from his mouth, tinted with blood.

"Rev—gather some snow for water. Carlos's horse needs it, and so does the boy."

There was no reaction. Ben turned and saw Duncan Warner sitting with his back against the cavern wall, his head tilted downward, his hat tugged over his eyes. Words began in Ben's throat, but he cut them off. Instead, he picked up the pot and walked toward the mouth of the cavern. *He better be praying,* Ben thought, *because if he's sleeping with that kid about to die . . .*

The pitch of the wind had changed from its manic howl to a lower, less-threatening key. The wind was strong enough to bite exposed flesh, but its intensity had waned. Ben crouched to jam the pot full of snow and then stayed in that position. He thought of how he had found Henry on the cavern floor. Had there been the smell of gunpowder then? He couldn't be sure—his nostrils had been plugged with snow. He couldn't have smelled a polecat if one had let loose in his lap.

Ben shoved handfuls of the fluffy snow in the pot until it was full, and then stood. *Whoever shot Henry must've ridden out into the storm. If that's true, the man is dead. No one could survive for more than a few hours out there. Unless, of course, he found shelter in a cave or came upon another cavern . . .*

When Ben came inside, the preacher was leaning next to Henry, his index finger gauging the throb of the neck pulse.

"How's he doing?" Ben asked.

Warner shook his head. "His pulse is slowing down, and it's uneven. And he's burning up with fever. The best I can do for him now is pray."

"Best anyone can do." Ben set the pot on the embers. "Soon as that's melted down, keep wiping his face. That might cool him a bit at least. I'm gonna take a look at Carlos's horse."

Rabbit was the name of the big bay Carlos had selected from the Busted Thumb string for the search. Ben recalled that Rabbit was dumber than a shovel of dirt but had heart and bottom and would go all day and all night without complaint. About six years old, Rabbit was tall and rangy, but his chest was broad and his muscles hard. Ben had backed the horse in a flat race against a heavy-set Appaloosa once; the bay had won him a piece of pie and a cup of coffee at the café.

Ben faced the rear of the horse and brought the injured left front hoof up and between his knees. He poked ice from around the frog of the hoof and picked at the crack a bit, cleaning away grit and ice. The hoof wasn't as bad as it had looked initially. The break began at the toe, swerved right an inch, and then continued upward toward the coronet—the hairline at the top of the hoof.

Ben eased away from Rabbit, letting the hoof free, and walked to Carlos's saddle. He found what he was after: a farrier's knife with a thick blade and a sharp hook at its end. He lifted Rabbit's hoof again, trimmed away some of the frog's tissue, and then used the hook to further clean the crack. There was a shard of stone jammed into the hoof wall about halfway up the separation.

Rabbit flinched as Ben got the hook under the bit of stone and snapped it out. The two sides of the fissure moved together immediately, the shape of the hoof seeking its natural configuration. Ben gave Rabbit back his hoof, but the horse still refused to put weight on it. There would be little pain now, Ben knew—but the horse didn't know that.

Ben walked around the horse and stood at his right shoulder for a moment. Then he butted Rabbit just as he would if he were forcing a locked door with his shoulder. Surprised, the horse squealed, tottered for a second, then put his left front hoof to the floor to keep himself from falling. As soon as he was balanced, he began to draw up the hoof, hesitated, and then put it down again.

"Nice work," the preacher called out from near the fire.

"He can't carry a man for a couple weeks, but the hoof came together real good. Like Carlos said, he'll be fine."

Rev Warner walked over to Ben and Rabbit. "I guess a man's got to know a little bit about a lot of things to survive out here."

A sudden groan from Henry brought both men to his side. Ben leaned over the boy and wiped his face with the cloth from his forehead. Henry's eyes fluttered open, closed, and then opened again. He focused briefly on Ben's face. "Preacher . . . the preacher," he whispered, his voice raspy and wet sounding.

"He's right here, son," Ben said, easing out of the way so Warner could take his place.

"Don't try to talk anymore, Henry," the preacher said softly. "I'm with you now. Close your eyes, and I'll pray over you."

The boy groaned again, barely louder than his whisper had been. His eyes quavered and then closed.

Warner began praying, his words too low for Ben to hear. But he could hear the tone of comfort, of caring, in Warner's voice. He suddenly felt like an intruder at a very private time, so he walked to the front of the cavern, forming his own prayer for Henry in his mind.

The storm's back was broken. The wind continued to swirl snow around, obscuring vision, but there was less of it falling. The tone of the wind had lost its stridency, and the lapses between the gusts were more frequent and lasted longer.

Night had fallen by the time Ben heard the report of a rifle. He grabbed his rifle and fired three times into the air as quickly as he could work the lever. An answering shot came clearly, almost undistorted by the now-faltering wind.

"Wrap Henry as best you can," Ben shouted to the preacher. "The wagon'll be here in a few minutes." He stood staring out into the glacial panorama, stunned by the beauty of it, even at a time of peril. The snow was sculpted into smooth, graceful peaks and valleys, and it seemed as if each individual flake was catching and reflecting the light of the moon and stars.

After a moment, he felt the preacher's hand on his shoulder. "Did you bundle up the boy? The—"

"There's no reason to hurry now," Warner interrupted. "Henry died a minute ago. He'd lost too much blood. But he died easy. Never opened his eyes and never spoke again—just stopped breathing."

The squeaking of the snow under the wagon wheels washed over the two men, one with his hands clasped in front of him, the other holding a rifle loosely at his side. Ben heard his horse's familiar long snort, and then

Carlos rode in with Lee, on Slick, at his side. They both swung down from their horses.

"Henry's gone," the preacher said.

"Oh, no!" Lee exclaimed, taking a step forward, her arms reaching out.

Who is she reaching out to? Ben couldn't help but wonder. He kept his eyes locked on her.

Lee suddenly lowered her arms. "He was so young."

Carlos nodded his head. "Ees sad," he said. "But Ben, we 'ave a herd of shopkeepers who're 'most frozen to death. If we go back thees night, we must start now."

The wagon pulled in and stopped behind Snorty and Slick. There were several horses tied to the back gate of the covered freighter. A half dozen men on horseback reined in and looked at Ben and the preacher with flat, emotionless eyes that seemed bright only because of the gray pallor of their faces.

Ben approached them. "You boys all right?"

It seemed like a full minute before one of the riders spoke. "We lost Zeke, Marshall. When the storm was real bad—jist 'fore we stopped—his horse dumped him an' took off. Zeke, he musta hit the ground hard. He busted his neck."

"Is his body in the wagon?"

The rider broke eye contact with him. "Nossir, it ain't. We had to leave him be, right where he was. We couldn't lift him, Marshall. Our hands was like boards, an' we didn't have no control over 'em. I fell straight down when I clumb off my horse, 'cause my legs an' feet are froze. Had a real hard time mountin' up again. I was scairt the boys was gonna leave me behind too."

Ben walked back to Carlos. "I don't see any sense in headin' back tonight. We've got fire an' water here, an' there's food and blankets in the wagon. Some of these fellas are going to lose toes—maybe fingers too. Another few hours in the saddle and it's a sure bet all of them will be frostbit. We can leave at first light tomorrow."

The preacher spoke up. "Marshall, you can't ask these people to spend the night in a cave with a dead body! I suggest we—"

Ben turned to face Warner. "It was another one of your suggestions that led to this, Rev. You might just be quiet an' follow orders this time around an' maybe we'll get past your little search party idea without no one else getting killed."

"Ben!" Lee gasped. "Duncan is a man of God! You can't speak to him like that!"

"He's a man of God, all right, and he's a fool too. It's a wonder there aren't more of you out there under a yard of snow."

Carlos eased his hand onto Ben's shoulder. "You say the truth, *mi amigo.* But now's not the time for it. We mus' get everybody inside an' beeld up the fire. We make coffee, Ben, *muy caliente* an' strong to melt a nail."

Ben hesitated for a moment and then forced a smile. "Very hot an' strong coffee is exactly what I need, Carlos. Let's get these folks inside. We'll put Henry in the wagon for the night. The cold won't bother him now."

The coffee was even better than Ben had anticipated. He sat with his back against the cavern wall with his second steaming mugful. Most of the stock of wood had been fed to the fire, and it roared high, casting light throughout the cavern and providing the lifesaving heat that was rapidly inducing the group to shed layers of clothing. More coffee was brewing, and its heady odor permeated the air, mixed with the scents of wet wool, wood smoke, and fresh hay.

The saddle horses and the pair from the wagon were twenty feet away, just inside the mouth of the cavern, pulling at the two bales of hay that had been scattered in front of them. Rabbit was carrying his weight on all four legs, moving normally and naturally as he shifted about. The search party had been forced back by the intensity of the fire, but they remained as close to the source of heat as they comfortably could, sitting with numb feet and toes extended toward the flames. A basket of bread, salted and smoked ham, jerky, and dried apples, almost full twenty minutes ago, was now down to scraps and bits.

Carlos hunkered down next to Ben. "The smoke," he observed, "it flew straight up an' out."

Ben sipped coffee. "Flew? Oh—flue. Yeah. There's a vent right above it that must go to the surface. We'd be choking like fish outta water if the smoke didn't have an escape."

"Ees good place for the night. But there still ees a *problema* though."

Ben nodded. "A big one. Who killed Henry?"

"Could be renegades. *Pistoleros*. Who can know?"

"Well, the boy couldn't have had much worth stealing. That ol' horse of his is gone and his saddle an' bridle too. But what bothers me is why the killer left into the teeth of the storm when he had a perfect hideout like this to wait out the weather. And why kill the kid? I doubt that Henry would've resisted much for that scruffy horse an' some broken down, secondhand tack."

"Those men, they don' need no reason to keel." Carlos paused. "You gonna talk with the preacher?"

"As soon as I can. I had no right to jump on him like I did, insult him to his face with everyone within hearin'.

Him being a preacher makes me even more wrong. I feel like a coyote for doing that."

"The search party—it was wrong. Zeke, he be alive if the preacher din't push heem an' the others to go out."

"Of course he would—but that ain't the point. I shouldn't have—"

"Marshall? A moment, please?"

Rev Warner stood in front of Ben and Carlos, Lee at his side. "I need to apologize," he said, "and I wanted Lee and Carlos to hear my apology. My search party was a fool's plan, just as you said it was. I should have listened to you right from the start." His voice carried a texture of remorse, and it impressed Ben that he spoke at a normal volume level, not whispering to save himself embarrassment. Ben's glance flicked to the group gathered near the fire. Conversation had died. Every pair of eyes was focused on him and the preacher.

Ben pushed himself up to his feet. "I'm the one who owes the apology here," he said. "You did what you believed God wanted you to do, and no one should ever be faulted for that."

Lee's eyes found Ben's, and there was a warmth in her gaze that seemed to have been absent in the past month. Ben looked back at the preacher and extended his hand. Warner shook it and let it go. There was a moment of uncomfortable silence until the preacher turned away and walked toward the fire, Lee with him.

Carlos, who hadn't stood, said, "Ees better, no?"

"Sure," Ben replied as he sat back down.

"*Mi amigo?*"

"Yeah?"

"His eyes, they don' apologize none."

"I noticed."

8

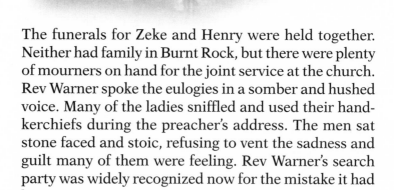

The funerals for Zeke and Henry were held together. Neither had family in Burnt Rock, but there were plenty of mourners on hand for the joint service at the church. Rev Warner spoke the eulogies in a somber and hushed voice. Many of the ladies sniffled and used their handkerchiefs during the preacher's address. The men sat stone faced and stoic, refusing to vent the sadness and guilt many of them were feeling. Rev Warner's search party was widely recognized now for the mistake it had been.

At the conclusion of the funeral service, Rev Warner again approached the pulpit. He faced the congregation for a long moment before speaking. "I feel directly responsible for the untimely death of Zeke Konrick," he finally said. "It is as if I threw him from his horse and then heaped snow and ice upon his dead body." There was a murmur in the pews, and the preacher waited it out. "I came to Burnt Rock with a joyous heart, burning with ambition, filled to overflowing with love for God and for those I'd serve here." He cleared his throat and took a deep breath, as if going on would cause him physical pain. "I've accomplished nothing here, beyond alienating the fine citizens of this town—a place I've come to love. I've brought justifiable wrath to our lawman, and I've led my friends and church members into a life-and-death situation in which they should never have found themselves. For that I'm deeply sorry."

The buzz from the congregation was louder this time, and it lasted longer. Again the preacher waited for silence. "This will be the last time I speak to you from behind this pulpit. I've shamed not only myself, but my calling and the work I've attempted to do here. Ladies and gentlemen—friends—I'm officially resigning my post as pastor of this fine church, effective immediately. I plan to move on tomorrow, and I pray that one day I arrive at a place where I can do God's work without my sinful nature interfering with—"

Missy Joplin was on her feet. "You'll do no such thing!" she bellowed. "We won't allow it!"

Others began standing, shouting out words of praise, of caring, of gratitude for the preacher. Lee stood. All the members of the search party stood. In a moment, the entire congregation was standing.

"Let's vote to refuse Rev's resignation," Missy yelled over the noise of the crowd. "Those who want our preacher to stay right here in Burnt Rock, shout out!"

It was the loudest blast of voices the small church had yet heard.

"An' now those who want Rev to move on, shout out now!"

The silence was that of a sepulcher.

125

The preacher looked over the group, meeting the eyes of many. He lowered his head for a moment. Then he raised it and looked over the people gathered in front of him. "Thank you," he said quietly. After a moment, he added, "I have work to do. Shall we adjourn to the cemetery to lay these two souls to rest?"

The day smiled upon the mourners. The sun, large and benevolent, turned the snow to trickles and freshets of icy water. Patches of buffalo grass were visible around the cemetery, and the snow that was loaded onto the boughs of the oaks and desert pines thudded to the ground as the heat released its bond to the branches. The sky was sweetly blue, much like the blue of an early June morning.

The open wagon carrying the two simple pine caskets was drawn by a matched set of black geldings owned by Uriah Root, the town undertaker. Most of the time, Uriah was probably the jolliest man in Burnt Rock. But on funeral days, his face was every bit as somber and bereaved as the deceased's closest relatives. He dressed completely in black, and the trappings and reins of his team were of black, highly polished leather.

A dozen men—three on each side of each coffin—lowered the boxes into the earth with stout lengths of rope. The handfuls of soil Rev Warner crumbled on the tops of the coffins made a lonely sound.

When the mourners had dispersed and Uriah's employees had begun filling in the graves, the undertaker approached Ben.

"I got a bit of a strange thing, Marshall," he said.

"What's that, Uriah?"

"Well, the thing is, when I was gettin' Henry ready for his coffin, I found four gold eagles sewed right into the lining of his coat. Seemed kind of funny. The boy never had no money, yet here he was carryin' eighty dollars an' wearin' a pair of boots that was worn clean through. Seems like he woulda bought himself some boots an' maybe better clothes. His wasn't far from rags."

"That's odd, all right," Ben agreed. He took up the slack in Snorty's girth and turned back to the undertaker. "Doesn't seem likely that Henry would be carryin' around that kind of money."

"Nossir. It sure don't. 'Course, some say Henry had fingers that was kinda sticky at times, but that's a lot of money. If he stole it, I think we woulda heard about it."

"Probably so. No one in town would lose eighty dollars an' not report it to me."

"Sure enough. I kinda thought I'd donate the money to the church without sayin' where it come from—maybe drop it into the poor box."

Ben considered this for a moment. "That'd be a right good gesture, Uriah. I . . . well . . . never mind. You go on ahead an' do what your heart tells you."

"You got maybe a better idea, Marshall?"

"Not better, I guess, but different."

"Well, out with it, then."

Ben moved a half step closer to Uriah, beginning a smile. "I was talkin' to Doc yesterday. You know how he treats for free folks who can't pay, right?"

"'Course I do. Everybody knows that."

"Well, the supply house in Chicago where Doc buys all his stuff—medicines an' so forth—has cut off his credit. He can't order from them without cash up front. I'd say that Doc's a man with a real need for that money."

"I'd say that too—and that's right where the money's goin'. I'll just give it unanimously, so's Doc don't know where it come from."

"Unanimously?"

"Sure. Mean's you don't know who done somethin'."

"I see," Ben said, trying not to grin. "Unanimous or not, I think you're doing the right thing, Uriah."

Deep winter settled on Burnt Rock and its environs like a washed-out blanket that had lost all its color during many trips to the boiling, lye-saturated water and the angry, crushing wringer that followed. Gray was the predominant color of the sky, and it was a flat, lifeless gray that seemed to paint the faces of the people in the same listless hue.

Ranchers sat in their kitchens, drinking coffee and pestering their wives. Their herds had been sold months ago, their barns and outbuildings were repaired, and their barbed-wire fences were stretched as tight as the string on a renegade's bow. A few hands stayed on to look after the herd of calves, but God had designed longhorns well. They flourished in conditions that would kill a horse and drain the life from a buffalo.

Farmers too sat in their kitchens, pestering their wives. Their plows were sharpened after the final turning of their acres, and spring seed had been ordered from the Montgomery Ward catalog. Draft animals grew fat and lazy from lack of use. Mules grew cantankerous and began tearing mouthfuls of hide out of one another in battles started by an accidental or purposeful nudge— or by nothing at all. When separated, the mules called back and forth to one another with voices so raucous and irritating that many farmers let their stock fight it out rather than listen to their caterwauling.

O'Keefe's Café did its best business of the year during the winter months. Bored men met there to drink coffee, discuss the weather, and play checkers. On the other hand, the Drovers' Inn languished, opening and closing many days without serving more than a half dozen drinkers. Gambling was on respite; the cardsharps and riverboat types found warmer places to practice their dishonest craft. And there were no incoming herds to fill the saloon with drunken, free-spending cowboys.

The celebration of Christmas provided the sole high spot of the winter. The Christmas service at the church was joyous and warm, and the children's traditional play was its usual success. But afterward, winter seemed to stretch into infinity.

Marshall Flood spent too many hours of his time sitting in his office, boot heels on his desk, staring at the wanted posters tacked to the wall. His paperwork was completely up to date, the cells clean, the office immaculate, and the floors scrubbed. He told himself that the daily rides on Snorty had the purpose of keeping the horse's strength up and his muscles tight. In actuality, Ben simply loved to ride. He was like a horse-crazy kid who'd saddle up his favorite mount and poke around for hours with no destination in mind.

On this day, the grayness was more pervasive than usual. There wasn't one spot of color anywhere Ben looked. The snow had gotten slushy due to a slight rise in temperature, and the sky appeared listless. Snorty, however, was happy to be out of his enclosure and argued with Ben for enough rein to allow a headlong run. Ben held his horse at a fast walk for a mile, feeling Snorty's muscles tensing under the saddle, and waited for the outburst of energy he knew would come. A long, head-shaking snort usually preceded such an explosion, just as it did this time. Snorty launched himself at the sky in a gigantic crowhop, bringing all four of his hooves a couple of feet off the ground.

Ben sat out the leap as if he were on a rocking chair in front of a comfortable fire, keeping the reins tight. Snorty hit the frozen, slush-encrusted dirt with all the grace of a dumped load of bricks, but Ben let his lower legs and feet absorb the thump. He snatched off his Stetson and whacked Snorty on the rump with it, and the horse responded with a series of angry crowhops that caused Ben to laugh out loud.

He hauled Snorty's head around, straightened him, and gave him all the rein he wanted. It took a heartbeat for the horse to realize that he was no longer held in check, then he threw himself forward, running for the simple pleasure of raw speed.

When the snow deepened as they galloped out of the protected side of a long valley, Ben eased Snorty down to a slow lope. The burst of speed and release of energy had been good for both horse and man. Ben felt much better—it was as if the rushing wind and exuberance of a fine horse had washed away the cobwebs and detritus of boredom.

As Ben headed back to Burnt Rock, he saw two horses approaching him from that direction. Even before he recognized the riders, his heart dropped. The tall, coal-black horse could only be Slick, and the gray riding next to him was Chowder, carrying Duncan Warner. As they drew closer, Ben's eyes darted to Warner's heels; there were no spurs attached to his boots.

Lee looked beautiful. Her cheeks were red with the cold, and the whiteness of her teeth flashed as she smiled and called out a greeting. Her hair tumbled down her back in wonderful disarray, its inky darkness framing her face. Ben felt an uncomfortable lump in his throat.

"You getting cabin fever too, Ben?" Lee asked, stopping Slick a few feet from Snorty.

The preacher offered a smile. "As much as I love my little home, I felt like the walls were closing in on me. My Sunday sermon isn't even half-written, but I had to go outdoors before I started talking to my furniture."

"I try to get out on Snorty every day for an hour or so," Ben responded. "My office gets awful small when there's nothin' much to do."

"Oh, Ben—let me tell you about the church social and dance," Lee said, a smile lighting up her face. "It'll be a cure for the winter boredom of all of us."

"Go on an' tell me then. I can use some of that cure," Ben said, returning her smile.

"Well, it'll be in Grange Hall next Saturday evening. We'll have a potluck dinner, and we've already got a fiddler and a guitar picker, and Doc's going to play piano. It'll be great fun. It was Duncan's idea. He thought a midwinter break might do us all some good."

"We'll put some flyers up around town," Warner added. "I think we'll have a real fine turnout." He smiled at Ben. "You'll be there, of course?"

"Sure." Ben forced the words from his mouth. "I wouldn't miss it." *'Course, I haven't danced since my third-grade teacher held a lemonade social.*

"Great. See you then. Lee—shall we get on with our ride?"

Ben's eyes met with Lee's. For a moment she looked flustered. Her gaiety seemed forced when she said, "I'll save lots of dances for you, Ben—and you haven't been out to supper in months. Please come by soon."

"I'll do that." He did his best to put a smile on his face, but his muscles wouldn't respond. He tipped his Stetson and cued Snorty as Lee and the preacher headed out.

The coffee in Ben's office had spent a bit too much time in the pot. It gave off a harsh, acidic scent, and when Ben poured himself a mugful, the tarry liquid moved thickly and slowly from the spout, flowing more like library paste than coffee. He sat behind his desk and drank it anyway.

He felt like he was under siege. He had a killer who may well have died in the storm—but he had no way to be sure the man was dead. If the killer had survived the weather, then he was a fugitive and it was a marshall's job to hunt him down and bring him in. *But where can I look for him? Scout all the caves and caverns of the foothills? Impossible. Wait until spring and see what's left of him? That doesn't make sense either.*

And Lee. What was happening with her? She was right; it had been almost three weeks since he'd ridden out to the Busted Thumb for a visit. Not that he hadn't tried, though. Ten days ago, he'd bought himself a bath and a shave at the barbershop, changed into fresh denim pants and a brand-new shirt, knocked the manure and mud off his boots, and spent a half hour polishing them. He'd gotten within a couple hundred yards of Lee's home when he saw Chowder standing at the hitching rail near the front porch. He had cut a tight U-turn and asked Snorty for speed before anyone saw him riding up. He'd spent that night playing checkers with Doc at the café.

The image of Lee earlier in the day with her red cheeks and her broad smile brought a pain to Ben's chest. When his mind replayed Lee and Warner riding off, his hands closed into fists. He didn't own Lee—he realized that. He hadn't even courted her properly. Instead, their lives had merged, and his feelings for her had grown, until he loved her more than he'd ever loved anyone in his life. But he didn't know if he could give her what she wanted and what she deserved.

He sighed deeply. "Ya know, Lord," he said out loud, "sometimes things get real tough. I'm feelin' like a kicked hound, an' I sure would appreciate some of your help."

When Missy Joplin came bustling into the office, she didn't, for once, barge through the door like a runaway locomotive. Ben's eyes snapped open from a semidoze, and he pulled his heels from his desk and stood, a smile on his face.

"Missy, seems like we haven't talked in a month of Sundays. Come on an' sit. I'll put some coffee on. What I'm drinkin' here is swill, but it won't take a minute to brew a fresh pot."

"You do that, Benjamin. I'll jist warm a bit by the stove. These ol' bones can't take the cold no more like they used to."

"You'll outlive the entire town, Missy."

"I sure hope not. I'm ready to go when my time's up. These winters try me terrible."

"Texas winters try everybody terrible. You're not the only one."

"No," Missy said with a grin. "I guess not. You goin' to the big social an' dance, Ben?"

Ben grunted noncommittally.

"Don't you grunt at me, boy. You'd best be there if you don't want to see your woman fly away."

"Missy . . ."

"And don't you *Missy* me neither. Lookit here, Benjamin Flood: Rev Warner is a fine man, an' he's sure got his eye on Lee. But Lee's heart is with you. You gotta do somethin' soon or she might jist give up on you."

"Do what? I ain't a preacher or even a gentleman, for that matter. Rev's got me outclassed."

Missy considered that for a moment. "You can't weigh dogs an' cats in the same scale," she said with a wave of her hand. "You're different kinds of men. Sure, Rev's smoother and prettier than you are, an' he talks just so, an' he always knows what to do to make a person comfortable. That ain't your way though, Ben. You're the type of man who won the war an' come West to open the frontier."

She sighed and then went on. "I done some thinkin' on this. Rev has become real important to me as a friend an' as a minister. I got a big place in my heart for him. When I first started seein' Lee and Rev together, I thought maybe it was a good thing. But then I got to thinkin' about how you an' Lee are together, an' that felt better to me. There ain't a thing I got 'gainst Rev, but you an' Lee seem right. See what I mean?"

"I dunno." Ben shrugged. "Are you sayin' the frontier needs both gunslingers and preachers?"

"Hush with that talk! You're no more a gunslinger than I am. What I'm sayin' is that you're a fella who gets done what needs to get done. It makes me right sad to see you let your gal get away."

Ben's shoulders drooped. "Makes me sad too, Missy. But I don't see that there's much I can do about it."

"There is, you know."

Ben placed the refilled coffeepot on the stove. "What?" he asked without turning to face her.

"You gotta quit mopin' an' start givin' Rev Warner some competition. The church social is comin' up—get you a fancy shirt an' a new pair of pants an' shave yourself smooth as an apple an' put on some bay rum an' dance Lee's feet offa her. Fetch her punch an' cookies an' pay all your attention to her. Make her feel right special, Ben—'cause she is."

134

Ben's face reddened. "I'm not much of a dancer, Missy. I never really learned it."

"Square dancin' ain't nothin' but learnin' a few moves an' listenin' to the caller. The waltzes an' so forth can get a mite tricky, but once you learn 'em, all you gotta do is shuffle round. You don't need all that fancy stuff. An' the truth of it is, three quarters of the men there will lumber round like wounded buffalo. You can't be no worse than they are."

"I suppose Rev knows dancin'."

"I 'spect he does."

"Uhh . . . Missy? Since you know all about it, I was kinda wonderin' if . . . well, if you ain't too busy, maybe you could teach me a little?"

"Now you're talkin', Benjamin Flood! 'Course I'll teach you some steps. You come by my place tonight after dinner, an' we'll get to it. You'll pick it up in no time."

"I'll do that, Missy. An' I'm gonna do somethin' else too. I'm goin' over to Scott's to buy me a suit of clothes. 'Bout time I had one, anyway."

Missy's face was suddenly that of a little girl who'd just gotten a fluffy kitten for her birthday. The lines that the years and the elements had etched into her skin seemed to be gone, and her eyes glowed. "You jist do that. Find you a nice suit that fits good an' polish up them ol' boots, an' Lee's heart will set to poundin' so loud you'll hear it over the music." She moved to Ben and took his hand. "Like I said, you an' Duncan is both fine men. But I've known you for some years, Benjamin. An' I know how Lee feels about you. In my heart, I've always seen you an' Lee together . . ." She moved closer to him. "Put your arm round my waist an' just move with me. We'll start your dancin' lessons right now."

135

Missy hummed a slow dance and pulled at Ben to follow as she executed a basic box step. Ben moved woodenly, as if his boots were planted in buckets of cement. Dots of nervous sweat appeared at his hairline.

"See? This ain't so bad, is it?"

"Well . . ."

"Just speed it up a little. Kinda ease me into followin' you. Good. Now I want you to turn me—you ease me along with your hand an' the arm round me, an' I'll go right round you. Ready?"

Ben hauled on Missy's waist as if he were bulldogging a steer, dragging her hand in his at the same time.

"Not so—ouch! Ya oaf! You ain't unloadin' sacks of grain, Ben!" Missy disengaged from his grasp and stood rubbing her hip where it had struck the corner of Ben's desk. Then she broke out into laughter. "Don't worry— I'm all right, an' you're doin' fine. I gotta run now 'cause I got a cake in the oven, but I'll see you tonight. A couple lessons an' you'll dance like you been doin' it all your life!"

As Missy spoke she surreptitiously rubbed her hip.

Scott's Mercantile was the biggest store in Burnt Rock, and it carried everything a person could need. The diversity of the stock—from patent medicines to books to plows to saddles—fascinated Ben. As usual, the wooden floors were perfectly swept, and the glass-front displays of handguns and hunting knives, husbandry equipment, pocket watches, and penny candy gleamed, spot and fingerprint free. The wooden stocks of rifles and shotguns glowed with polish, and the pleasant scent of gun oil hung in the air. The smell of good leather and neat's-foot oil around the dozen or so stock saddles set on sawhorses was fresh and clean and brought a smile to Ben's face. Bits were arranged in a display case, in graduated sizes and types from the basic bar bits to snaffles and cutting-horse bits with copper ports that helped to generate saliva in a working horse's mouth.

Ben stopped in front of the patent medicine display to read a few titles. Lydia Pinkham's Compound for Women was a big seller, and Mr. Scott kept a few dozen bottles on hand at all times. There were cures for catarrh, nervousness, cancer, goiter, toothache, general debilitation, alcoholism, sleeplessness, headache, myopia, trembles, sadness, and a number of other problems and diseases Ben had never heard of. Each potion claimed to be 100 percent effective when used as directed, and each was a compound of "special" ingredients found in no other medication. Ben picked up a bottle of Dr. L. H. Dupont's Positive Cure for Smoking and Craving of Tobacco. Its price was eighty cents. Ben himself had given up the habit, but he wondered why a man who enjoyed a cigarette or pipe or cigar would spend almost a dollar trying to quit something as harmless as smoking. The fact of it was that Bull Durham and other tobacco, cigar, and cigarette makers spoke of the healthful and relaxing effects of the habit.

Tremont Hildebrand hustled up behind Ben. "Not feeling well? Anything I can help you with? I'm sure something here will take care of what's bothering you."

Ben turned and shook hands with the head clerk and mercantile manager. "I'm just lookin', Tremont. I'm feelin' fine. What I'm after today, though, is a good suit of clothes that won't cost me too much."

Tremont Hildebrand was the sort of person who appeared to be moving even when standing still. He was thin, clean-shaven, and impeccably dressed, as always. His shoes were polished until they reflected light as well as any mirror, and the crease in his trousers was sharp like the blades of the German-steel straight razors he sold.

"There's no better investment for a man than a good suit, Ben. You're in luck too. I just got a shipment of men's suits all the way from Rochester, New York. They're quality goods, and I'm able to give you a good price on one."

As they moved toward the back of the store, Tremont flicked bits of almost invisible dust from items on shelves. He crouched in front of a bundle of spades and shovels and used his white handkerchief to erase a finger smudge from the blade of a long-handled manure scoop. The aroma of mothballs and fresh fabric welcomed them to the long line of men's suits hung on wooden coat hangers from a stained and polished three-quarter-inch wooden dowel. Tremont stood back from Ben, appraised his size, and selected a suit.

"You'd look good in this one," he said.

"It's kinda . . . well . . . *bright,* isn't it? Kinda shiny?"

"That's the style. All the rage in Paris." They moved a few feet, and Tremont selected another. This suit was dark and had a very simple cut. "Try on the coat," he instructed.

Ben pulled the garment on. The sleeve length was approximately correct, but the material seemed to hang on him, the shoulders loose and the lapels narrow and limp. Ben shrugged his shoulders. "Leaves me room to get to my pistol," he commented.

"Always a consideration, of course. It's a conservative suit. Stylish yet understated."

"Awful dark is all."

"But excellent for legal duties and so forth."

"Excellent for an undertaker too. Let's try one that's a bit more cheerful."

Tremont moved down the line of suits, his hand cupping his chin as he studied the colors and fabric. "Here it is! This is called a pinstripe. It's the newest thing. Lots of famous men wear this style—William Cody, politicians, and the like. Try on the coat."

The suit was a somewhat dusty-looking color with faint chalky stripes. The coat fit Ben a bit better than the earlier one had, but it still seemed to balloon out from his shoulders.

"Put the trousers on to get the full effect," Tremont suggested.

Still wearing the coat, Ben walked into the changing room, pulled the door shut on the tiny cubicle, and tried on the trousers. They sagged at the rear, but the waist fit snugly. He went back to the selling floor. "Can you take up the rear, Tremont? Looks like I'm carryin' a sack of coal back there."

"Of course—it won't take but a few minutes. You like it, then? Is this the one you want?"

"I like it well enough, I guess. How much is it?"

"As I said, you're in luck. You can have the suit for fourteen dollars. I'll do the alterations for free."

Ben began removing the coat. "Too rich for my blood, Tremont. I'll go change out of the pants."

"I want you to have that suit," Tremont protested. "It's perfect for you. How much were you thinking to spend?"

"I figured maybe a total of eleven dollars, includin' a good shirt."

The head clerk looked aghast, as if he'd been cruelly insulted. "A suit like this for eleven dollars? Impossible. Absolutely impossible. Mr. Scott paid more for it than that. But look—as our lawman you deserve a discount.

I'm giving away my profit, but you can have the suit for thirteen dollars."

"Twelve including the shirt."

"Twelve fifty. And I'm robbing my own employer at that price."

"Done," Ben said. "Let's take a look at your shirts."

Grange Hall looked as it always had from the outside: a wooden frame structure painted white, without even a suggestion of a frill to break up its stark linearity. It was a large building, big enough to contain grange offices, with a large, open, wooden-floored area used for events such as speeches, demonstrations of farming techniques, cattle and sheep shows—and church socials and dances.

Inside, there was nothing left of the raw function-over-form of the place. Cloth streamers in a range of gaudy colors hung from the rafters and moved with the breeze that snuck in with every arriving person. A fire roared in the stone fireplace, sending waves of heat through the central open space of the building. Long tables had been set up for the meal, and each was laden with what looked like enough beef, ham, bread, potatoes, cakes, jams, jellies, and miscellaneous treats such as corn fritters, honey-drenched cookies, taffy, and thickly frosted cupcakes to feed an artillery division. There were four large coffeepots suspended from the support in the fireplace, and a massive punch bowl rested on the main table, filled with a mixture of sarsaparilla, candied fruits, and fist-sized chunks of ice.

Children ran about as children do, laughing, hollering to one another, the boys paying special attention to the table with the cookies and taffy. Older youngsters—

most in their early to midteens—stood around in self-imposed segregated clusters of boys and girls.

The women of Burnt Rock wore whatever finery they owned, with long, petticoated skirts swishing around them as they walked. When Lee entered the room, shaking the light snow from her hair, Ben found he couldn't answer Doc's question about the quality of the past summer's hay. The ebony sheen of her hair fell well below her shoulders, cascading down the whiteness of her dress. Her face was red from the cold, and she was laughing at something Missy had just said. The black-diamond luster of Lee's eyes seemed fathomless. For a moment Ben felt as if he could fall into them and never return to the surface. He had heard of a person's heart skipping a beat, but he'd never experienced it before. Now he knew what it felt like.

"Ben? What're you gawking at? Have you been paying attention?" Doc turned and saw Lee approaching. "I see," he said, making an unsuccessful attempt at hiding a grin. "She's a stunner, all right. Well, I'll see you a little later." Doc patted him on the shoulder and moved toward a group of ranchers discussing the merits of the fancy new Angus breed versus the longhorns.

Lee stopped a few feet from Ben and took a long look at his suit. "You look so handsome," she said. "That's a fine suit—makes you look like a teacher or a lawyer."

"You're the one who's looking real good, Lee," Ben said. "Like Doc just said, you're a stunner."

Lee laughed easily. "That Doc is a flatterer. Everyone knows that."

"Still, what he said is the truth."

"The truth? Did I hear someone mention the truth?" Duncan Warner came up from behind and smiled at Ben and Lee, taking and releasing Lee's hand and then shaking Ben's. "You're looking glorious tonight, Lee," he said. "May I bring you a cup of punch?"

"Please do, Duncan. Something cold will taste good."

Ben watched as the preacher turned and strode toward the largest table, stopping every few feet to greet someone or to respond to a greeting. His suit, properly dark in line with his calling, fit him perfectly. Where Ben's coat gapped at the back of his neck, Warner's rested smoothly. Although Tremont had removed quite a bit of fabric, Ben's trousers still hung loosely. His boots almost sparkled with polish, but he noticed that the preacher was wearing actual shoes that caught and flashed the light from the dozen or so lanterns hung about the room.

Lee must've been following his eyes. "It's not the clothes, Ben. It's the man who wears them that counts. Duncan has spent time in cities and you haven't, but I'll tell you this: You're the best-looking man here."

Ben's face colored. He didn't know what to say. "And you're the finest and prettiest lady, Lee," he finally said, looking into her eyes. "Do you want . . . no, I mean, may I have the pleasure of your company for dinner?" The line sounded contrived to his own ears, but Lee's response was worth the embarrassment.

"You may indeed. It'd be my pleasure, sir."

When Ben saw the preacher headed their way with a cup of punch in each hand, he touched Lee's arm and gently guided her to the table where the plates, utensils, and napkins were waiting. She didn't see Rev Warner stop midstride and watch her, or the quick ember that flared in his eyes, but Ben did—and it made him feel good.

9

The young girls of Burnt Rock hauled the empty bowls, platters, plates, cups, and utensils to the sink in the rear of Grange Hall. They chatted with one another as they found unnecessary tasks to do nearest the tables where the young boys sat with their parents.

The adults, sated and happy, drank coffee and visited, watching the musicians assemble their equipment around a somewhat battered old piano on a slightly elevated platform in a rear corner of the open room. The only members of the church missing from the crowd were Carlos and Maria, who'd taken advantage of a break in the weather to visit their son, daughter-in-law, and first grandchild.

The guitarist, a tall, muscular fellow with long, graying hair, sat on a wooden chair, tuning his instrument. The left leg of his trousers was pinned up to just above where his knee would've been—he'd lost a leg to a Federal charge at Second Bull Run. Next to him stood the fiddler, sliding his bow carefully across a lump of rosin. He too had fought at Bull Run—as a Union sharpshooter.

The guitarist picked up what appeared to be a metal frame from the floor next to his guitar case and fit it over his head. He took a C chord harmonica, slid it into the frame directly in front of his mouth, and blew gently into it. Heads of those nearby turned toward him. The sad moan like that of a midnight train cut through the talk and quiet laughter of the crowd.

Rev Warner approached the musicians, a mug of coffee in his hand. He nodded to them, smiling. "My name's Duncan Warner," he said. "I'm the preacher here. We're very grateful to have you. I've heard great things about your music."

"Caleb Goode," the guitarist said, offering his hand. "And this here is Hank Dalton," he added, gesturing to the fiddler.

"Pleased to meet you," Warner said. "I understand you're just passing through Burnt Rock."

"Yep," Hank answered. "We come to see my niece an' eat a score or so of her fine meals on our way by. We got some jobs lined up for us down the road. When Julie— she's my niece—asked us to stay on an' play her social, why, we leaped at the chance."

Caleb was sliding his left index finger into an amber-colored cylinder about three-and-a-half inches long. Warner watched curiously. "What's that?" he asked.

"It's part of the neck of a whiskey bottle. It's called a slider. I can get some great sounds outta my guitar when I press it against the strings." He settled his guitar in his lap, finger-picked a few chords, and then eased the slider down almost to the base of the neck. The resulting music

144

went from the gentle patter of melodic rain to an earthy howl and then back. "See what I mean?"

Warner smiled. "I've never heard anything like that. Is it your idea?"

"Nope. Was the slaves who first used a slider, playin' their work songs an' spirituals an' such. Some of them men can make a guitar talk an' tell the saddest stories in the world. It's from them I learned about usin' a slider."

The smile on Rev Warner's face faded. "You won't be playing any of that slave racket tonight, will you?"

Caleb met the preacher's eyes. "We sure are. Fact is, right before we do some of them songs, we'll tell the crowd you requested 'em."

"The war's long over, sir," Hank added.

"Of course it is," Warner said. "No offense, gentlemen." He turned away and almost bumped into Lee and Ben.

"I hope you're not too full of dinner to do some dancing, Duncan," Lee said. "I saw you packing away Harriet Shippet's cake and ice cream."

"A man can never be too full of fine food to dance," Warner replied. "And I'd be very proud if you'd allow me the first dance of the evening."

"That's a great offer, Duncan, but I think Ben . . ."

"You go right ahead, Lee," Ben said. "I've already promised the first dance to a right fine lady, an' she was kind enough to accept."

Lee's eyes narrowed. "I see," she said.

"Yes ma'am, Missy Joplin tol' me she'd do me the honor if I promised to keep my boots off of her feet."

Lee laughed prettily. Warner chuckled too. "I didn't realize you were such a dance floor sort, Ben."

Ben held his smile. "There's lots of things you don't know about me, Rev."

145

Ben was awkward for the first few moments on the dance floor, but the gentle rhythm of the music soon captured him, and he and Missy moved almost effortlessly through the simple steps he had learned.

"You're doin' jist fine, Ben," Missy whispered. "I'll allow that it was kinda like teachin' a one-legged calf to walk when we started, but you done good."

Lee and Rev Duncan glided by as if their feet weren't touching the floor. They moved to the music so naturally that other couples missed steps as they watched. Ben tried not to notice.

The first square dance was a simple one, beginning with the men lined up side by side, with the ladies a few feet away, also side by side. Doc called out the steps and moves in a voice he reserved only for such duties—loud, penetrating, full of fun. The second dance was considerably more complicated, and a few times Ben and several other men found themselves standing alone, outside the rhythm, wondering what to do next. But the orphans soon found their way back into the caller's instructions.

After an hour or so of dancing, Caleb sang a few English ballads, accompanying himself on his guitar. "Barbara Allen," a frontier favorite, held the audience enthralled with its simple but poignant lyrics. "Old Blue," a Kentucky hunter's song about the death of a good and cherished dog, had the men choking back the knots in their throats and the women reaching into their sleeves for their handkerchiefs. The next two songs were at the opposite end of the scale: "Froggy Went A-Courtin'" and "Chuck Wagon Stew" restored the air of festivity and fun.

It was when the musicians took a break that Ben smelled the first sign of trouble. As he filled his and Lee's punch cups, the thick, woody scent of whiskey reached him. He looked around the room but saw nothing amiss.

146

He handed Lee's filled cup to her. "Did you . . . ?" he began.

"I smelled it too," Lee said, nodding her head. "Everyone knows the rules."

"Yeah. I better circulate a bit, see what's going on."

Ben moved easily through the crowd, speaking to a friend here and there, his eyes constantly in motion, seeking out faces he either didn't know or didn't expect to find at a church social. His first concern was weapons. As far as he knew, he was the only armed man in the hall. Church rules stated that no side arms or concealed guns could be carried at any function, and the men in attendance had complied, just as they always did. But as Ben walked around the dance floor, he passed through several waves of alcohol-tainted breath that clashed with the scents of coffee, lilac water, and ladies' powder.

He found at least eight intruders and perhaps a couple more. Two cardsharps from the Drovers' Inn smiled with red-rimmed eyes, their gaudy gambler's suits and oiled hair setting them apart from the farmers and merchants. Several cowhands who'd hung on in Burnt Rock after their herds were shipped moved through the room. The lumps pressing against their shirts at the waistband were as obvious as a mountain cat on a dance floor.

After Ben had circled the room twice, Doc approached him with Rev Warner a foot behind him. Lee followed the two men. "What's going on, Ben?" Doc asked, his voice lowered.

"Must be a dull night at the Drovers'," Ben replied. "That place has been as quiet as a tomb for weeks. Looks like business is pickin' up, and a few of the lowlifes decided to come an' pay us a visit."

Doc sighed. "They're not here to do-si-do. What're you going to do? Should I get some of our men together?"

Ben shook his head. "We'll have a pitched battle here if you do. They're carryin' guns and they're drunk. I'm gonna try to reason with them, maybe talk them into leaving. There's no reason for a fight here. If they stayed in that swill-pit down the street where they belong, we wouldn't have this trouble."

Rev Warner put his hand on Ben's shoulder. "Marshall—let me go around and talk to them. I'm sure I'll be able to get at least some of them to listen to reason."

Ben shook his head. "They won't listen to you. Most of them are afraid of me—maybe they'll back down. You don't know men like these, Rev. They came here to—"

"They're here because trouble is what they live for," Doc interrupted. "There's not a one of them who wouldn't stomp on a wildflower just because it's pretty."

Lee stepped closer to Ben. "Why not let Duncan try? It might help, and it can't make things any worse than they are."

But Ben had already started moving. "Won't work, Lee. This thing feels like it's right at the flash point. I want you to find Missy and then both of you get out. Do it as quick as you can." He hurried to the stage, opening the buttons on his coat as he did so. He took his badge from his pocket and pinned it on his chest as he stepped up onto the platform, rapping sharply on the top of the piano with his knuckles.

The room fell silent except for a raucous burst of laughter from three men standing together at the rear of the dance floor. Nervousness and apprehension spread through the congregation like poison in a waterhole. All eyes locked on Ben.

"There are a few boys here tonight who don't know our rules," he called out to the room. "This here's a church social. There's no reason for a man to be armed, and we don't allow alcohol. I'm gonna have to ask you boys who've been drinkin' and carryin' guns to leave. I don't want trouble, an' these good people don't want trouble. There won't be any if you men leave now. Go on out the door, an' we'll forget the whole thing."

"What if we decide to stay?" a rough voice shouted out. "What then?"

"We jist come to do a little dancin' an' Bible readin', Marshall," another voice shouted. "Maybe have a glass of your nice punch, though some of us, we like our sarsaparilla straight. Nothin' wrong with that, is there? Say, and ain't you Bible-thumpers always tryin' to drag people into your church? Sure you are. An' now that we come, you get all testy on us. Jist don' seem fair, Marshall."

Hoots of laughter and frightened glances between members of the congregation filled the room for a moment. Ben pushed the side of his jacket back behind his holster and put his right hand an inch from the grips of his Colt.

"I've got nothing else to say, an' I won't stand still for you mocking these people. I want you out—now!"

The lantern hanging above and behind Ben exploded as he finished his sentence. Burning kerosene cascaded to the floor and puddled there, its flames reaching hungrily for more fuel. Two other lanterns, hung directly on the walls rather than from the rafters, showered the room with flaming shards of glass as gun shots echoed through the hall.

"Out! Everyone out!" Ben bellowed.

Pistol fire continued from the dance floor, and three more lanterns spewed kerosene. Again Ben shouted, but the warning was ineffectual; his voice was swallowed by the screams of women, the shouts of men, and the

149

hiss of the conflagration. A cowhand took aim at a lantern, and Ben dropped him with a single shot.

The fire was a voracious, living thing, glutting itself on the wooden structure. Lanterns assaulted by tongues of flame detonated like bombs, accelerating the propagation of the inferno. Thrashing, screaming knots of people jammed against one another at the front and rear doors of Grange Hall. Ben ran to the door closest to him and began dragging men and women away from the door frame as if he were pulling and throwing away dried corn stalks in a field. After clearing away the people to the safety of outdoors, he stepped back inside, looking across the room through the sheets of flame. Doc and a couple of other men were hustling people through the front door.

On the far side of the room a gambler aimed a derringer at one of the two remaining lanterns. Ben ran toward him, and his hoarse bellow caused the gambler to spin around. The gambler's single-shot pistol swiveled toward Ben, but a slug from Ben's Colt put the gambler on the floor.

Ben knew it was too late to do anything about the building. The roof was on fire. He looked around the room frantically, his eyes smarting and tearing from the thick, acrid smoke.

Doc's voice reached him from across the room. "Get out, Ben! Everyone's out!"

A rafter dropped onto the top of the piano with a whoosh. The last thing Ben saw before he plunged through the door to safety was a finger of flame emerging from the sound hole of Caleb Goode's guitar.

A head count outside revealed that everyone except the outlaws Ben had traded shots with had gotten out of Grange Hall. There was a halfhearted attempt to form a bucket brigade, but it was clear that buckets of water would have no effect on the blaze.

The flashes of orange and red and cobalt blue bursting forth from the collapsing structure seemed eerily cheerful; the sparks and embers rising into the inky blackness of the sky flashed like Fourth of July rockets.

Women, their long dresses singed and burned, their faces smudged with soot and tear streaks, stood wide-eyed, clutching children in iron grips. The men stood about silently, their Sunday meeting suits stinking of smoke and panicked sweat. Some brushed with their hands at the ragged scorch holes in their clothing. The children seemed numb with shock. A few of the toddlers—and a few of the grade-school children—screamed hysterically, hiccupping and gasping.

Lee, Missy, and several other women stood huddled together. Ben, eyes streaming tears and still gasping from the smoke, stepped in front of the group.

Lee met his eyes with a level, frigid gaze. "You should've let him try, Ben, but you had to bull ahead and get up on the stage and incite those animals to start shooting."

Ben had no idea what was she was talking about, but then the preacher's plea came back to him. "He couldn't have done a thing!" he choked out. "What happened in there," he nodded toward the fire, "was planned. Those drunken fools came with the idea in mind to shoot up those lanterns. Rev Warner would have gotten a few punches or maybe a few bullets for his trouble, and the outcome would've been the same."

"You don't know that." Lee's words were coming fast now. "You could've let him try. But you had to pin on that badge like it was a shield of a knight in armor and take everything into your own hands!"

151

Ben looked into Lee's eyes and again saw an expanse of arctic ice. He turned wordlessly and strode to where his horse was tied. Some of the horses had bolted in panic—one hitching rail was torn away, and a pair of broken reins hung from the top rail of the fence of the grange's small corral. But Snorty, breathing as if he'd just completed a hard run, had stood his ground where his master had left him. Ben swung into the saddle and rode toward town.

Main Street was dark except for the yellow light issuing from behind the batwing doors and the front window of the Drovers' Inn. Ben tied Snorty in front of his office, unlocked the door, and stepped inside. He didn't bother lighting a lantern. The subtle glint of moonlight on the rack of rifles and shotguns gave him all the illumination he needed. He tugged a Remington twelve-gauge double-barreled shotgun from the rack and jerked open the drawer at its base so hard that the drawer pulled free of its tracks and spilled handfuls of 30.06, 30.30, and 44.40 cartridges at his feet. He loaded the shotgun's twin barrels and picked through the ammunition on the floor, stuffing six or eight shotgun loads into the ripped pocket of his new suit.

He left Snorty where he was and walked down the sidewalk to the far end of Main Street. Drunken hilarity reached him when he was twenty yards away. At ten yards, the heavy, stomach-wrenching reek of cigar and cigarette smoke, whiskey, and the sweat of bodies long unwashed struck him like a slap in the face. He strode on.

He stepped through the batwings and stood silently, shotgun angled across his chest, its stock resting in his left hand, his right hand at the breech. At first, none of the dozen or so men in the saloon noticed him—and then all of them did. Conversation, laughter, and general racket stopped. When Ben pushed the safety lever of the shotgun to the off position, the oiled click seemed as loud as the clang of a blacksmith's hammer on an anvil.

"You can't come bargin' in here with a shotgun, Flood!" the bartender called out, reaching for the army Colt he kept under the bar. "We got a legal business here, an' you got no right to—"

"Where are they?" Ben shouted, his voice still heavy from the smoke. "An' if you pull that gun you're reachin' for, it'll be the last thing you do."

The bartender stepped back and placed both his hands on the bar in front of him. "Where's who?" he asked, the beginning of a smirk on his face.

Ben scanned the fifteen or so men at the bar and at the tables, cards clutched in their hands, bottles, glasses, paper money, and coins scattered in front of them. He didn't see the men who'd burned Grange Hall, but he hadn't really expected to. Like vermin fleeing a prairie fire, they'd fled from the flames and, no doubt, from Burnt Rock.

"I'm lookin' for the cowards who tried to burn to death a lot of innocent people tonight," Ben said. "The arsonists are from the same litter you pigs are from. They were here guzzlin' booze before the fire."

"Way I heard it," the bartender said with a grin, "one of them lanterns jist up an' busted into flames. Terrible accident. Them Bible-thumpers, they gotta learn not to overfill their lamps. Funny, though—you'd have thought that God, why, he'd come rushin' on down and put out them flames."

Ben let the shotgun hang from his right hand, the barrels pointed downward. "Funny," he said, matching the bartender's grin, "that Satan ain't gonna come up from hell and save all the poison you've got here."

153

Tipping the shotgun upward, he fired from the hip and squeezed the two triggers at the same time. The shelves of bottles at the near end of the bar erupted like a volcano, spewing whiskey and shards of glass. The men hit the floor. Ben broke the breech of his weapon, dumped the spent shells, and inserted two fresh ones in one quick, smooth, well-practiced motion. With the next blast, he took out the shelves of bottles at the far end of the bar. Again, while the thunder still lingered in the air, he reloaded and squeezed off two more shots at the six untapped wooden barrels of beer stacked against the wall in two tiers of three across the room. Streams of beer flowed like miniature waterfalls to mix with the whiskey, dirt, and glass on the floor. Ben shifted the shotgun to his left hand and drew his Colt with his right.

A half-full amber bottle on a table became fragments, and its contents slopped over a cardsharp cowering on the floor. Two rounds sent a pair of spittoons clattering, their viscous contents leaving a thick trail. His final three shots riddled the face of a roulette wheel, splintering it and filling it with holes.

Ben holstered his pistol, looked over his handiwork through the thick cloud of gun smoke, and backed out the batwings to the street.

Early the next morning, smoke from Grange Hall permeated the air of Burnt Rock. The blaze had long since died, but here and there in the blackened pile of scrap lumber that smoldered where the building had once stood, wisps of smoke still rose.

Doc pushed a thick crust of bread across his plate at the back table of the café, guiding the last couple of bites of scrambled eggs to his fork. Ben sat across from him, a mug of coffee in his hand.

"Think you'll get any legal trouble from the owners of the Drovers'?" Doc asked.

Ben shrugged. "They know if they pull anything like that, I'd start patrollin' that hole a half dozen times a day. Fact is, I'd kinda like to do it anyway."

"Like it or not, drunkenness and gambling are legal, Ben."

"Public drunkenness isn't legal, and crooked gambling isn't either."

"No," Doc agreed. "It isn't. I guess they'll let it lie." He sipped coffee and then asked, "Have you seen Lee? She was awful upset. Why she laid into you like she did, I don't know, but I'm sure she didn't mean what she said."

"Well, I'm not real sure about that. But I do need to talk to her. I'd like to ride out to the Thumb this afternoon."

"Good idea. I'd hate to see you two separate because of something like that."

"I would too. But there's a bit more to it."

Doc sipped again, hesitated, and went on. "Reverend Warner?"

Ben pushed back his chair and stood. "I got work to do, Doc. Thanks again for all the help last night. Without you and a couple of the others, the whole thing would've been a lot worse."

"Wish I could've done more when the shooting started," Doc said. "You take care, my friend. Give my regards to Lee."

Doc's eyes followed Ben to the door. After it had closed behind him, Bessie walked over to Doc's table and sat down. "Is he all right?" she asked.

"I'm not sure," Doc said. "I asked a stupid question I shouldn't have."

Bessie was silent for a moment. "About Lee and the preacher?"

155

"Yeah."

"Ben's gonna lose her, Doc. Unless he does something, he's gonna lose her."

Doc sighed. "I know."

A couple of dreary days later, the sun made one of its rare winter appearances as Ben saddled Snorty in the enclosure behind his office. The somber gray of the sky was chased away by the yellow disk and replaced with an azure expanse that assured the world that winter wouldn't last forever.

Snorty's hooves raised spurts of slush and water as he loped toward the Busted Thumb. Bits of soil and patches of dead buffalo grass appeared as the snow receded under the sun's power, and the air was redolent with the scent of decaying weeds and grass and the fresh smell of melted snow and thawing soil.

Ben reined in and dismounted halfway to Lee's house and checked the set of Snorty's shoes. Prairie mud was referred to as "the blacksmith's friend" because there was nothing better to suck shoe off of a hoof. Snorty's hooves were fine, the shoes tight and the nails holding perfectly. Ben remounted and rode on.

He had no idea how he'd be received. Lee hadn't come to town since the night of the fire. Of course, that wasn't unusual. Still, he was worried. *"But you had to bull ahead and get up on that stage . . ."* repeated like a litany in his mind. And it wasn't just Lee's words that he couldn't forget, but also the fear and, perhaps, the disgust he'd seen in her eyes. He shuddered, although the sun was warm.

When Ben arrived at the Busted Thumb, Carlos was in a training pen with a two-year-old dapple-gray mare, exercising her on a line, clucking at her when she slowed from the lope he wanted her to hold. He waved to Ben. "Good to see you, *amigo!*" he called.

Ben rode up, ground tied Snorty, and climbed up the fence to sit on the top rail. "She moves right pretty," he said. "Little stumpy in the pasterns, but she carries herself good."

"We can no breed her 'cause of the pasterns. Thees mare, though, she got more cow sense than most of our studs. Heart too. Ees a good horse."

"How's little Juan? Got him in a saddle yet?"

Carlos beamed. "Soon. He ees no but two month old. One day Juanito weel own much land an' many fine horses. Thees I know to be true."

"I don't doubt that for a second. Miguel an' Yvonne are good?" Ben asked.

"My son, he choose a bride sweeter than clover honey. That ees why they make so grand a baby, no? They both good an' asked after you."

"I'll tell you what, Carlos—one day I'm gonna lock up the office an' ride on down there an' visit with them for a few days an' eat till I fall over an' not do a lick of work."

"You should do thees, Ben," Carlos said seriously. "Miguel an' Yvonne, they love to have you." He whistled, and the mare backed down to a walk. He walked to her head and rubbed her muzzle. "You have trouble while I wass gone?"

"Some. Nothin' I couldn't handle."

"The fire, it wass a terrible thing. Thanks be to *Dios* no one died." He paused. "An' you shoot up the saloon?"

"Sure did. How'd you hear?"

"Some of the men, they were at the fiesta. They tell me when I get back early thees morning. You could no wait till I could come with my rifle and *pistolo*? You hurt me, my friend."

157

"It needed to be done right then, Carlos. Next time I'll come for you. All right?"

"Ees good. Amigos, they should take their fun together, no?"

Ben nodded, then paused before saying, "Lee around?"

Carlos didn't meet his eyes. "She out on Slick."

"Alone?"

Carlos inspected the ground between his boots. "No. The preacher, he ees weeth her."

Ben eased down from the fence. "Tell her I stopped, Carlos."

"Ben—Maria will make coffee for us, no? We talk a bit?"

"Another time. I've got work to do. Give Maria my regards, hear?"

Carlos stood next to the mare, rubbing her flank absentmindedly as he watched his friend ride off. After a minute, he led her out of the pen and toward the barn.

10

Missy Joplin's home was a reflection of the lady herself—warm, welcoming, comfortable, and without pretension. Although she was the wealthiest resident of Burnt Rock, very few in town or even in her church group knew of her funds.

"More tea, Lee?" Missy asked.

"No—no thanks. I've got to be getting back to the Thumb. I'm not even sure what I rode to town for. I don't have any real business here today." She sighed.

"Trouble, honey?"

"Yes. Duncan and Ben. Ben's acting like a schoolboy with a crush, and Duncan's . . . well . . . Duncan. He's polite and sophisticated and treats me wonderfully. But there's something about Ben that stays with me. You know what I mean?"

"'Course I do. They're both good men. I don't think I'd like to be in your position, honey—havin' to choose betwixt an' between. Each of them has jist a ton of qualities. Now, Rev, he knows things that Ben don't—about money and so forth. But Ben has that kindness about him that he seems to try to hide. Why—"

"Money? What do you mean?"

Missy sat a bit straighter and captured Lee's eyes with her own. Her voice dropped almost to a whisper, although the women were alone in Missy's house. "Not a word 'bout this to nobody, now. You promise me?"

"Sure. But what do you mean?"

Missy grabbed Lee's hand. She seemed as proud as a youngster with an important secret. "Rev is willin' to let me in on a land operation that'll triple my money in a matter of a few months. It ain't that I need the money to live, but my plan is this: I'll triple what I have an' then give it to the church at the time of my passin'. Wouldn't that be grand? Makin' sure the church doesn't have any financial problems for years an' years?"

"That's a wonderful thought, Missy. But what kind of land deal are you talking about?"

The widow's eyes sparkled. "See, me an' Rev Warner have gotten to be good friends. We talk a lot over coffee or tea. Rev knows lots of rich men from when he was in Dallas, an' they offered to let him in on the whole thing. It's right-of-way land that a new railroad company needs to buy. The plan is to buy it up now, real cheap, an' sell it back to the railroad at a good profit."

"I didn't know Duncan had a ministry in Dallas. He never mentioned it to me," Lee said.

"'Course he did! He had him a big church an' all, but left 'cause of that poor, sorry sister of his in Chicago."

Lee thought for a moment. "Missy—how much are you thinking of investing in this thing?"

"That plain ain't your business, honey. It's between me an' Rev. I'm right grateful he brought me the opportunity." She smiled proudly. "Don't you go thinkin' I'm too old to know a good chance when I see one."

"I wasn't thinking anything like that, Missy. It's just that there's a lot of money involved, and I don't want you to get hurt."

Missy shrugged away Lee's concern. Her voice suddenly became hard. "Are you sayin' you're scared Rev Warner is tryin' to trick me into somethin' shady?"

"Not at all! I'm sure Rev is giving you what he believes to be excellent advice. It's just that . . . well, he's a minister. Even though he knows some wealthy men, he's still a man of God and not a financier. See what I mean?"

"There's times when we got to trust those we believe in, Lee." Missy's voice wasn't exactly cold, but it lacked the warmth it usually conveyed.

Lee squirmed in her chair. "Look, suppose I run the plan by the town attorney and ask his advice. I won't mention any names—in fact, I'll tell him it's something I'm looking into. That won't be a lie—I will be looking into it, right? Just give me the name of the railroad and the group buying up the—"

Missy pushed back her chair and stood facing Lee. "You gave me your word on this. I'll 'spect you to keep it. This deal is fragile, an' if too many people start snoopin' around, the whole thing will fall apart. That's exactly what Rev Warner told me. An' I believe him, whether or not you do!"

"It's not a matter of not believing Rev, Missy! I'm just trying—"

"I'm sorry, I jist can't talk about this anymore. I have things to do, honey. Thanks for stoppin' by." She led Lee to the front door. The customary hug they exchanged there was strained. When Lee pulled away, she could see the hurt in Missy's eyes.

Lee tightened the cinch and swung into Slick's saddle. There was little traffic in town, and she jogged her horse to the point where Main Street ended and the open prairie began. The gray sky around her seemed to reflect the condition of her heart. She put Slick into a lope and pointed him toward her ranch.

The usual exhilaration of riding her prime stallion was absent. The rush of the wind, the cadence of Slick's hooves, the communion between horse and rider were chased from her mind by the words she'd exchanged with Missy Joplin.

Lee reined in a few miles outside town, wanting some time to think. She climbed down from Slick's back, leading him by a single rein as she walked. The ground was slightly soft, and the dead weeds, scrub, and buffalo grass were muted colors, sad remnants of the green that carpeted the prairie in the spring and summer.

I promised not to discuss the deal with anyone. But what if there's something wrong? What if Duncan misunderstood what his friends told him? What if he simply didn't understand the facts? Another thought pushed those thoughts away. *Why has he never mentioned being in Dallas to me?*

Lee stopped, her eyes closed. *Lord, I need your counsel. In the past you've always pointed me in the right direction. Please come to me, Lord, and whisper into my heart what I should do.*

When she stepped into her stirrup, her decision was made. She believed that a promise is a sacred thing. But merely talking to Duncan wouldn't be breaking the promise she'd made. After all, he was already privy to all the facts.

When she arrived back at Burnt Rock, she could see Duncan through the front window of his home. His eyes and hands were focused downward, although she couldn't see what he was doing. Her face eased into a smile. *Looks like he's reading—probably the Bible. This man I almost doubted is reading the Bible.*

She tied Slick to the rail in front of the preacher's small porch and climbed the three steps to the door. She could hear him moving about inside, and she knocked on the door, the smile remaining on her face. She wondered if she'd share her concerns about the land deal with him, and then quickly decided that doing so would be unnecessary.

The preacher smiled broadly at her as he opened the door, words of welcome on his lips. "Lee, how good to see you! Please come in and chat for a bit."

She followed Duncan into the living room. His large, leather-covered Bible was open on the table where he'd been sitting.

"Please, sit," he said, pointing to an armchair. "I've got a pot of coffee on. Will you have a cup with me?"

"I'd like that. Thank you." Lee settled into the chair.

"I'll be just a moment. I'm sorry I can't offer you anything to eat."

"Coffee will be fine. I had a big breakfast with Carlos and Maria this morning, and a bite with Missy not long ago."

When Duncan left for the kitchen, Lee looked around the tidy room. The wood of the table holding the preacher's Bible gleamed warmly, as did the mantle over the fireplace and all the other wood in the room. A strange but familiar scent reached her nose. She sniffed in but couldn't identify it. It was a bit like neat's-foot oil, but that wasn't quite it.

Slick snorted outside, and Lee rose and walked to the window. A boy on the other side of the street was rolling a hoop with a stick, and his dog was running alongside the metal circle, challenging it to a fight. She watched for a moment until the boy, dog, and hoop turned up an alley and Slick settled down. As she moved away from the window, she noticed that the Bible was open to Psalms—and that it was upside down on the table.

Lee returned to the armchair as Duncan carried in a small wooden tray with a pair of coffee cups on it. He offered the tray to Lee, and she took a cup and sipped at it. "Mmmm," she said, "nothing like fresh coffee."

"Yes, I agree," the preacher said as he sat down at his table, putting his tray near the Bible.

"Reading the Good Book upside down, Duncan?" Lee asked, smiling. "Is that a new way to study Scripture?"

"What?" the preacher snapped. He looked down at the Bible, and his face suffused with red. "Oh—I must have turned it when I got up to go to the door." He looked away from the book and into Lee's eyes. "I'm sorry I barked like that, Lee. I've been under quite a bit of pressure lately. Please forgive me."

Lee felt her face redden too. "Certainly," she said. "No harm done." She cleared her throat. "Say, what's that smell I noticed? It's something familiar, but I can't quite place it."

The preacher sniffed the air. "I don't smell anything, but it could be the furniture polish. Missy was here yesterday, and she cleaned up a bit."

"That's probably what it is," Lee said agreeably, even though she was quite sure the scent wasn't that of furniture wax. "Actually, it's good that you mentioned Missy, though, because she's why I'm here. And, of course," she added diplomatically, "a cup of your coffee and a chance to visit with you."

The preacher waited expectantly, without speaking.

Lee cleared her throat. "Missy told me about the investment she plans to make. I'm not sure that she completely understands all the details, so I stopped by to discuss it with you."

Duncan's smile seemed forced. "I told her not to . . . well, the poor lady does tend to forget details at times. That's why I didn't want her to talk to others about it." He sipped his coffee. "It's quite simple, actually. Several rather wealthy friends of mine have formed a consortium to purchase land that they know will be bought within a few weeks by a new railroad. Of course, the group will buy the land for little more than pocket change per acre and sell it back to the railroad as right-of-way for a very sound profit. That's all there is to it."

"Why the secrecy, then?"

"Well, think about it, Lee. If the fact that the railroad is going to buy the land gets out, speculators from all over would be buying it up, planning to do exactly what the consortium is."

"I guess that makes some sense. Still, it's not the sort of thing I can see Missy involved in. I . . . I just don't feel right about it. It's not that the plan is dishonest, but it seems like the group is taking undue advantage of the railroad, somehow."

"Business is business, Lee. Think how wonderful for the church it will be after Missy passes on."

Lee felt uncomfortable at the implication behind his words. "How much is Missy going to invest?" she asked.

The preacher shifted in his chair. "I can't—won't—answer that. Missy specifically asked me not to reveal that to anyone. But I can tell you this: I know that the bank draft has arrived from Boston, closing the account where Missy's husband had his investments and savings."

165

"She's investing everything her husband left to her?" she asked. "But what will she live on!"

Duncan stood. "She has plenty of money here in the Burnt Rock bank to provide for the rest of her life." He paused. "I'm sorry, Lee, but I won't discuss the matter with you any longer. You're asking me to breach the trust of a dear friend, and I won't do that."

Lee stood too. It was obvious the meeting was over. "Thanks for the coffee," she said. "And for your time."

The preacher walked her to the door and accompanied her outside. As she mounted Slick, she asked one more question, struggling to keep her voice neutral. "Did you ever have a church in Dallas, Duncan?"

He answered her smoothly. "Poor Missy—another thing she doesn't understand. I never had an actual church in Dallas, but I worked among the poor there."

"But if you were working with the poor, how did you meet the wealthy—"

"Thanks for stopping by, Lee. It's always a pleasure to visit with you." Duncan turned away and climbed the steps to his front door before she could respond.

Lee was in sight of her ranch when the scent she'd been wondering about came to her mind.

It was gun oil.

Warner watched Lee ride off. After she had disappeared, he shoved the chair she had been sitting in and then kicked it, for no reason other than it felt good. "Nosy shrew of a woman," he muttered. "Just like all women—can't keep her snout out of places where it doesn't belong." He kicked the table, and the Bible thudded to the floor, its pages fanning like wings. Then he bent to pick up what he'd been forced to hide under the chair when Lee rode up.

166

The hard rubber grips of the Colt .45 revolver fit his right hand perfectly. Just holding the pistol helped him think more clearly. After all, the gun had been a genuine friend. It had saved his life twice during the war, and then many times in lousy little cow towns so insignificant that he couldn't remember their names.

The barrel gleamed as he turned the weapon over in his hand and admired the simple, deadly mechanics of it. When he spun the cylinder, the soft whirr of the action brought a smile of pride to his face. The brass tips of the six bullets he'd barely gotten loaded into the Colt before Lee came storming into his home glinted warmly in the light from the window. He set the pistol aside for a moment and picked up the tooled leather gun belt and holster, brushing bits of rug lint from it as carefully as a mother arranging a newborn infant's hair.

He looked out the window. There was plenty of light left, and he didn't have to ride far to get out of hearing range. He needed some time outside the squalid little town and the drab little people who inhabited it. He needed some time with his best friend.

Warner buckled his gun belt around his waist and tied the piece of latigo around his leg to secure the holster. He let his fingers graze the grips for a moment and then took a long duster from his closet and shrugged into it, checking to make sure the long tails of the coat completely covered his weapon.

Chowder cringed to the back of his stall when Warner opened the gate. After backing Chowder into a corner, he jammed the bit into the animal's mouth. He tossed his saddle blanket onto Chowder's back and followed the blanket with the saddle. Then he kneed Chowder sharply in the gut and hauled the cinch tight before the animal could inhale.

As he rode toward the end of Main Street, Mrs. Bartlett, a member of the congregation, called out to him from the sidewalk. "Hello, Reverend! I just baked a pie. Would you care to join me for a piece?"

"I can't stop, Julie," he responded, trying to keep his voice pleasant. "I'm going on a sick call. Sorry."

The sucking of the glutinous mud tired Chowder quickly. Warner pushed the horse, mumbling curses, and lashed the reins back and forth on the sides of the horse's sweat-slick neck. When Chowder began breathing even more loudly than the thoughts tumbling in his mind, he reined in near a rise that was scattered with rocks and some larger boulders. He dismounted, wrapped the reins snugly around a hip-high boulder, and tried to calm his own breathing. If he came apart now, he knew, the whole package would be gone. The money from the old woman, the money he knew was in Lee's safe, and the entire performance he'd been giving for what seemed like an eternity.

He could feel all his hard work falling apart. Lee would figure things out quickly, particularly if she got Missy to talk more with her. Was the rest of the facade strongly enough in place? For the moment, anyway, he believed that it was. But the whole thing was like a long line of dominoes standing one behind the other. If one was tipped . . .

His act had been good. After all, he'd perfected it in the last two churches he'd been involved with. *There's always one believer who has a lot more money than the others. Always. And this stupid old woman is the richest yet.*

What he had learned at that seminary school his parents had sent him to years ago had helped him through some scrapes. It certainly helped with talking to those Bible-thumpers in Burnt Rock. He had the old lady believing every word he said, even about the land deal fraud. Still, he'd made mistakes. Paying off that kid had blown up in his face.

The storm had stepped on his idea to bring the boy back to Burnt Rock as if he, Warner, had found him. That would have reinforced his credibility with the people in town and made him even more of a leader. Maybe even a hero. But when the kid started whining about more money, there was no other way to go—he had to be eliminated. The fact that the bullet didn't do the job almost gave things away. If Flood, that lovesick puppy of a lawman, had half the sense of a stray mule, he'd have seen what Warner was up to. That thieving weasel of a kid wasn't calling for the preacher—he was trying to tell Flood that the preacher had shot him.

Warner shook his head like a dog shedding water after a swim. Enough thinking. He unbuttoned and removed his duster and tossed it over a nearby boulder. A sensation of peace came over him. The gun belt around his waist felt good. He shifted his stance slightly, his boots a foot and a half apart, his right foot a few inches ahead of his left.

Bits of mica in a bucket-sized rock thirty feet ahead caught his eye. His weapon leaped into his hand as if by its own volition. Six bullets sculpted the rock, smashing into it, creating fissures and faces that spun away, whining in a high-pitched scream. Fine bursts of brown dust rose when each slug struck the rock, but the bullets hit the rock so fast and in such a tight cluster that the grit rose as a single small cloud.

He clicked open the cylinder and dumped the empty casings at his feet. As he reloaded, the warmth of the oiled metal brought a smile to his face. He put six new rounds into the pistol and selected a smaller rock, farther out. His smile spread as he watched the rock skip about, growing

169

smaller each time he hit it. When he picked up the jagged, marble-sized nub that the rock had become and sent it whistling off into the prairie, he laughed like a child.

When all the cartridge loops in his gun belt were empty and his Colt reloaded, Warner felt as refreshed as a man who'd just bought a long bath and a close shave at a barbershop. His mind was no longer scrambling. He knew precisely what he needed to do. It was time to finish up in Burnt Rock. Besides, he didn't think he could stand to preach one more sermon.

He holstered the pistol and put on his duster. Chowder attempted to back away from him as he approached, but the looped reins around the boulder held the animal securely. He mounted the horse, dragged his head around toward Burnt Rock, and jabbed heels into his sides.

Warner tied up behind Missy's house. He didn't want a passerby—or the old woman herself—to see that his horse was lathered and dripping sweat.

Missy greeted Warner at the front door. "I'm so glad to see you," she said. "I've had nothin' but trouble today."

"What's the problem? If I can't help you, the Lord certainly can." He noticed that her eyes were red and puffy. "Let's go inside and sit down and you can tell me what you're upset about."

Missy tried a smile that didn't work. "Let me take your coat, an' then I'll fetch us some coffee. Or do you want tea? I have both."

Quick sweat broke out on his forehead; he'd forgotten that he was wearing his weapon. "Tea would be fine," he said. "I'll leave my duster on for a moment. I got a little chill riding here." He sat in a straight-backed chair in the parlor; his Colt and holster felt like an anvil strapped to his leg. He adjusted his coat carefully. Explaining to the old crone why he was armed would take longer than it was worth.

Missy returned with two cups of tea. She handed one to him and then sat on the sofa. Again, she tried to produce a smile, with the same poor result.

"Tell me, Missy," he said gently.

"It's about the investment and my money. Rev. Lee was here. She as much as said right out that I'm a crazy ol' lady for doin' what I'm doin'."

Warner feigned surprise. "How can that be?"

Tears began to seep from the old woman's eyes, and she brushed them away with the back of her hand. She choked on a sob and then said, "I tol' her about it. I know you didn't want me to, but Lee promised not to tell anyone else." She met his eyes. "It's the right thing, ain't it? What we're doing is jist and godly, ain't it?"

"Of course it is, Missy." Warner was silent for a moment before he spoke again. "I hate to say this, but I'm very concerned about Lee and the influence Ben Flood has over her. I'm afraid that her faith is failing and that she's following a bad path that will lead her straight to perdition. I've seen for myself that the marshall is a violent man, and I'm worried what effect his sins will have on her. I . . . I hesitate to even think of what goes on when those two are alone together."

Missy brought her hand to her mouth. "Rev—you can't mean that! They're good Christians, and they're my friends. I know them. You must be mistaken!"

He shook his head slowly. "I'm sorry I have to tell you this, but I've seen them together. I rode up one evening to the back of Lee's house. They were drinking whiskey—they had a bottle right on Lee's kitchen table. They were drunk, laughing like fools, and . . . and kissing. They were kissing, Missy, and not like friends kiss. I was so shocked that I rode away."

Missy began crying, and her voice broke as she spoke. "Oh, Lord. I never thought . . . what can we do? How can we help them?"

"We'll pray for them, my dear. And there's one other thing we can do to show them what real faith is, how real Christians follow the true path the Lord set out for us." He waited a moment and looked down at his hands.

"Please," Missy sobbed. "I'll do whatever it is. *Please.*"

Warner paused, as if thinking. "What we need to do," he said in a level, calm voice, "is to go to the bank right now and have the document signed directly over to me. I'll send it right on to Dallas. Then we'll call the congregation together and tell them exactly what we've done— and why we've done it. We'll show Ben and Lee that we don't only talk about faith and charity, but we act on it. They're bound to be moved back to the Lord's side by that."

Missy was on her feet. "Yes!" she exclaimed. "Let's do it, Rev! Let's do it right now!"

"You're completely sure, Missy?"

"'Course I am, Rev! If you'll hook ol' Muffin to my surrey, I'll run a brush through my hair an' be ready to go."

Missy scurried from the room, so Warner went out through the back door to the small barn where Muffin, Missy's cart horse, was kept. Muffin watched him from her stall as he pulled the light, two-passenger surrey outside. He arranged the reins along the traces and went back inside to bring Muffin out. He'd driven Missy's surrey once a few months before, and the mare remembered him. When he reached for Muffin's head in the stall, she spun away, snorting nervously. He cursed, shoved past her shoulder, and clutched her ear in his fist, twisting it sharply. Muffin squealed but stood still. Warner jammed the bit in her mouth and banged it painfully over her teeth. The mare squealed again, and sweat broke out on her neck and chest. Her eyes were wide with fear as he reached to buckle the strap over her muzzle, and she snapped her head back, away from his hand. Warner snarled a curse and threw a powerful blow to her face.

"Reverend Warner!"

He whirled around. Missy stood in her best coat, her hands in a rabbit-fur muff. Her eyes were as wide as those of her horse, but with a difference. Muffin was frightened, but Missy was angry.

"The horse attacked me, Missy. I had no choice but to defend myself!"

"Muffin has never attacked anythin' but a flake of hay in her entire life! I won't tolerate animal abuse from anyone, preacher or not." She glared at him, and her words trembled with anger. "I'll ask you to leave my property, Rev Warner."

"You can't—"

"I most certainly can throw you off my land! I have no use for any man who treats a horse as you jist did my Muffin. Lee may well have been right about you, sir. I'm gonna have to rethink this whole arrangement. And I'm gonna talk to Lee and Ben about it."

Warner cursed again and dragged the tails of his duster apart. Missy gasped as he drew his pistol. "Your friend Lee is my next stop after the bank. That safe of hers is just bulging with money, I've heard. And you're not thinking anything over, you pathetic old fool. You're going to do exactly as I say. If you don't, you won't be doing any more Bible-thumping. I guarantee you that."

"You're a whitened sepulcher, *Mr.* Duncan Warner, if that's even your name." Missy's words dripped like venom from a snake's fangs.

173

Warner replied in a controlled voice. "You're going with me to town," he said evenly. "You're going to sign the document with me. You're going to act calm and natural in the bank, or I'll kill you right there. Understand?"

"All of a sudden I understand a lot of things," Missy said. "I ain't goin' anywhere with you. Do you think I'm afraid of your gun at my age? I've lived my life. I'm ready for whatever comes—even if it's at the hands of a Judas!"

Warner glared at the old woman. "You'd make things a little easier being with me. That Turner is nosy. But the letter I wrote to Boston specified that the draft should be payable to either or both of us. Turner's bank has no say in the matter. The draft is legal. They have no choice. You'd have made things look a little better, but that's all. And if you'd started to flap that big mouth of yours . . .well, I guess it's better this way."

"Ben Flood will track you down and make you pay for this. He—"

Warner laughed. "I've faced better men than Ben Flood. He's nothing, old woman." He stepped closer to Missy and raised his Colt. "I guess I don't need you any longer."

"Rev Warner, good to see you," Sam Turner said. "Come right in. Have a seat." The bank president ushered him into his office, then went back to the big leather chair behind his desk. He rubbed his arm as he sat down.

"That arm giving you trouble again, Mr. Turner?"

"A bit, Rev. Winter seems to bring out all the old aches and pains in it." He rubbed the arm again and added, "It's a souvenir of a bank robbery a year ago. Ben and Doc saved my life then, you know."

"So I heard, sir. Terrible thing. We'll say a special prayer for you Sunday."

174

"Prayers are always appreciated, Reverend. Thank you." Sam paused. "What can I do for you today?"

"Well, I just left Missy," Warner said. "She insisted that I have the draft made payable to me, withdraw it, and forward it immediately—today." He grinned. "When Missy gives an order like that, a man doesn't have a chance to argue with her."

Sam looked perplexed. "Forward it to whom?"

"I'm afraid I can't tell you that, Mr. Turner. It's a business opportunity Missy wants to invest in." He smiled again, holding the bank president's eyes. "I'll give you my word as a man of God that I've investigated the company and its board of directors carefully and that it's entirely valid and aboveboard. There's absolutely no risk to Missy. I'm even putting some of what little money I have into it."

Sam didn't return Warner's smile. "Frankly," he said, "I'm not at all comfortable with doing what you ask, Reverend. We're dealing with a very large amount of money here."

Warner's smile disappeared. "You do know, don't you, that under the law I have every right to demand the bank draft. I'm not a fool, Mr. Turner. I know that you have no choice but to do what I ask—comfortable or not."

Sam stared at him. He slowly reached over for a small silver bell sitting on his desk and shook it. Marcia Hildebrand, a bank employee, appeared in the doorway of the office.

"Mrs. Hildebrand," Sam said, "I need you to prepare a bank draft, please. Pull the Hannah Joplin/Duncan Warner file and work directly from that. I need the full amount of the funds made payable directly to Duncan Warner." He looked again at Warner. "Please wait at the cashier's window. We're finished here."

11

Ben's office was growing smaller with each moment he sat at his desk. The walls were closing in like a vise, and the inky, smudged faces on the WANTED posters seemed to smirk at him, goading him to do something.

But what?

He'd seen Missy in the café earlier that day; she'd seemed subdued, hesitant, as if she were concealing something. Such behavior was out of character for the elderly widow, and it bothered him. Missy had been his friend since the day he rode into Burnt Rock. He'd eaten at her table more times than he could count, and he thought he knew her pretty well. There was something very wrong, and it boiled like water in a cauldron, just below his consciousness.

His thoughts shifted to Rev Warner. Something about the man had been bothering him for a while now, something he remembered seeing at the preacher's welcoming party. When Buck Starrett's rifle went off, the preacher had moved to his right simultaneously with the report from the street. His right hand had darted toward his side; then he'd stumbled over. Or pretended to stumble. Was the man just frightened of the unexpected roar of a gunshot? Or was the move an instinctive gunfighter's reach for a pistol?

And then there were the cruel cuts on Chowder's sides. The search party debacle. Henry's murder.

Ben sighed. He knew full well that his own jealousy of Warner entered into the mix.

He stood and walked to the coffeepot. The semisludge that remained in the bottom of the pot was as thick as horse laxative, and probably, he imagined, about as tasty. He glopped some into his mug and drank it down.

He paced out of his office and into the cell area, walking quickly but not going anywhere. He went back to his desk and sat down again.

He couldn't turn off his thoughts. Suppose Rev Warner was playing the entire congregation and the whole town as a pack of fools? What would make so many months of posing and lying worthwhile? And if Warner was a fake, he was awfully good at playing the part he'd chosen. His sermons had moved the entire congregation— including Ben.

He fidgeted with a pencil, tapping its point on the surface of his desk in a mindless rhythm. When the point snapped, the small cracking sound seemed to echo through the office.

His last meeting with Missy came to his mind again. *She can't tell a lie—her eyes give her away. But what was eating at her? Was she afraid of something or someone? Was she sick? Was she simply lonely?* Another thought

177

pushed its way into his head. *When was the last time I stopped by her house?*

Ben dropped the pencil on the desk, stood, and reached for his hat.

Ben swung Snorty to the back of Missy's house and, startled, drew rein more quickly than he'd intended to. Her surrey was just outside the barn, the lines rigged and ready for a horse, the traces resting on the ground. The fenced corral where Missy turned Muffin out in good weather was empty, and there was no sound of any kind from the barn. Even old Muffin in her stall didn't greet Snorty with her usual squeal.

Ben dismounted and left his horse ground tied. No light shone from Missy's house, and the barn was dark too. He touched the grips of his Colt and walked to the front of the barn. He waited for a moment until his eyes adjusted to the thicker darkness. To his left, Muffin was in her stall, facing away from him, as if she were trying to push her way through the corner to the outside. Muffin was a friendly old mare—always had been. Something wasn't right.

The barn wasn't a large one. It had a single box stall, a tack room, and storage for hay and grain to the rear. The surrey, when not in use, fit neatly in front of the pile of baled hay. There were two windows on each side, but they were dirty with hay dust and dead flies, and admitted little light.

A lantern hung to his left. He took it down and reached up to the beam under the lamp, searching for lucifers. His fingers found them. He struck one and lit the lantern.

At first, the white bundle adjacent to the hay appeared to be a heap of clothes. But the splash of red that caught

178

his eye indicated the form was much more than tack-cleaning cloths or discarded garments to be used for rags.

Missy was on her side, her face away from him. He eased her gently onto her back and sucked in a breath when he saw the laceration across her forehead. His fingers searched her throat for a pulse. When he found it—faint and erratic—he whispered his thanks aloud.

Missy's face was cold under his fingertips. The wound on her head continued to bleed, but slowly and thickly. The wintry air had helped to partially seal the laceration with clotted and frozen blood. Ben gently allowed Missy's head to rest on the dirt floor of the barn. Then he stood and backed away a couple of steps before spinning around and rushing to Muffin's stall.

The old mare was trembling, and the salty scent of her fear-generated sweat filled Ben's nostrils. He spoke quietly, mostly nonsense words and sounds, before stepping inside the stall. The gate wasn't latched—Muffin could have bolted if she weren't so frightened.

He stroked the mare's muzzle, still talking to her. He hated to waste time, but he knew it was better to calm Muffin now than try to wrestle her between the traces in such a spooked condition. After what seemed like a day and a night, Muffin's trembling quieted and then stopped. He led her to the surrey, buckled the surcingle—the band around her belly and over her back—around her, and fed the lines through the brass rings. Muffin grunted happily; this was all familiar to her. Ben knew that she now felt secure.

He threw a couple of blankets behind the seat of the surrey. When he picked Missy up, her lack of weight startled him. But he felt the small warmth of her back against his arm, and when she moaned quietly, his hopes surged. He placed her on one of the blankets and tucked the other around her. Then he fetched Snorty, tied him to the back of the surrey, and climbed up to the driver's seat. When he swung the wagon around, Muffin responded as smoothly as a fine watch, picking up her carriage-lope immediately.

Most of Burnt Rock was closed down for the night, but there was light in Doc's window—a providential light. Ben began bellowing when he was still thirty feet away.

The physician met him as he pulled up in front of the office. He hushed Ben with his hand as he looked over Missy. "Inside," he said as he spun on his heel and hustled into the dispensary. Ben followed, gently cradling Missy.

"Out," Doc grunted as Ben eased her onto the wooden examination table. Doc was already washing his hands at the sink as Ben stepped through the door to the waiting room.

Rather than sit and count the seconds, Ben drove Missy's surrey to the livery stable and saw that Muffin was put up for the night. The air was colder now, and the night was fully dark. Stringy clouds scudded past the almost full moon, and the stars seemed close enough to pluck out of the sky, like ripe apples from a tree.

Doc came into the waiting room shortly after Ben reentered the building. "She's going to make it," he said, before Ben could ask. "She took a real bad hit on the head, but she's a tough old bird. She lost more blood than I like to see in someone her age, but she's going to be all right. She has a concussion, but it doesn't seem like a bad one, at least at this point."

Ben released his breath in a long, satisfying whoosh.

"There's no possibility that it was a fall. There are bruises on her arms, most likely from someone grabbing her. Any idea who did this to her?"

Ben shook his head. "No. Who in the world would do that to a sweet ol' woman?"

"Well, did you go into the house? Maybe she was robbed."

"No—I didn't have time to check. When will she be able to talk?"

"Probably as soon as she wakes up and gets oriented to where she is. That's always a shock when a person is knocked—"

"Doc! Doc!" The voice from the dispensary was hardly that of an injured geriatric patient. "Fetch Ben!"

Ben and Doc stood still for a moment, looking at each other, then rushed into the back room. Doc moved to Missy's side, gently pushing her back to a prone position.

"You stay flat now, Missy. Ben's right here. What's the—"

Missy's eyes were somewhat dulled by the sedative Doc had given her, but her feisty spirit still burned behind them. She looked up at Ben, who was bending over her, his hand touching her shoulder.

"It was the preacher, Ben! He's a fraud and a liar, and he's on his way to Lee's house to get the money in her safe!"

Before Missy could say more, Ben was out of the room, freeing Snorty's reins from the hitching rail in front of Doc's office. He vaulted into the saddle and asked his horse for everything he had.

Carlos tugged against the ropes that held his wrists behind him. He spat a mouthful of blood at Warner's feet. "You peeg! You theenk you win over Carlos by sneaking up like a snake? Cut thees rope an' we see who ees a man!"

Warner pulled the bandanna from around Carlos neck, formed it into a ball, and stuffed it in the man's mouth. "You know, Mex, you always did flap your jaws too much. You're not worth killing, but you're sure worth shutting up."

Carlos tried to blink some of the fuzz from his vision. He hadn't heard Warner approach him from behind in the main barn, and the whack on the top of his head with the butt of a pistol had knocked him silly. When he had awakened, he was in the tack room, trussed like a hog. Now he lay still, thinking. It was time to wait. As soon as Warner left, he would begin pounding his boot heels on the floor. The noise would be sure to attract one of the hands—they walked back and forth in front of the barn on their way to the bunkhouse. Again, futilely, he strained at the ropes.

Carlos heard Warner's footsteps toward the front of the barn. He forced himself to wait another full minute and then began slamming his heels against the wooden floor, wrenching his tightly tied legs up as high as possible and then crashing them to the floor. The noise was hollow-sounding but loud. It was sure to attract attention. Sweat broke on his forehead. He pounded the floor even harder.

Suddenly the darkness was pierced by a dim light. Warner swung the door all the way open, a lantern hanging from his hand. "Not awfully smart, are you, Mex? You think I'd walk away without seeing what you'd do?" He drew his pistol and flipped it in his hand so that the butt faced forward. He stepped closer to Carlos.

Carlos looked at the phony preacher, refusing to give the man the satisfaction of seeing his eyes close before the blow struck.

Lee stood in the kitchen working the pump handle to sluice water over her supper dishes. She gazed out the window above the sink, wondering what Carlos was up to in the main barn. He was the only one who had any reason to be there, and she'd watched his lantern moving around, into the tack room, out to the front of the barn, and then into the tack room again. Now the light was moving toward her house, and she smiled. She needed someone to talk to; Carlos would do just fine. She wiped her hands on a dish towel and stepped over to the back door, swinging it open.

"C'mon in, Carlos. I was just wondering . . ."

Warner stood in the doorway, smiling at her. "Not expecting me, Lee? I'm hurt that you'd prefer that fat old fool to a man of the cloth."

Lee stepped back and raised her hand to her mouth. "Duncan! What on earth . . . ? I don't know what's gotten into you, but whatever it is, I don't like it at all." She began pushing the door closed, but Warner shoved through and stepped in, slamming the door behind him.

"What do you think you're doing?" Lee shrieked. "I want you out of my house right now!"

"I can't say I care at all about what you want. And I just want one thing: I want you to open that nice little safe you've got in your office."

"My safe? Duncan—what's going on with you? I—"

Warner grabbed her arm and began hauling her toward her office. "You must be as simpleminded as your Mex friend. I want your money, Lee—and that's all I've ever wanted from you."

He hung the lantern on the hook inside the small room that served as Lee's office. Under a library table covered with mare and stallion breeding records, feed bills, and circulars and folders announcing horse sales around the West, sat a dull gray safe.

"Open it."

"You're a total fraud, aren't you? You're no more a preacher than my horse Slick!"

"I sure did convince you and all your church friends, though, didn't I? Now I've got the old lady's note that'll turn right into money wherever I go, and I'll add yours to it."

Lee was silent for a moment, then spoke in anguish. "All this time you lied to us. All the while you've been here, you've been playing us like a fish on a line."

Warner nodded, and when he spoke, his voice was light and conversational. "Did real well, didn't I? I even had you looking doe-eyes at me, dreaming of marrying up with a preacher."

Lee glared at the man, her voice becoming arctic. "You're assuming an awful lot. I never saw you as anything but a friend. Why, Ben Flood is twice the—"

Warner took a long step toward her and slapped her across the face. "Open the safe. I don't have any more time to waste." His voice had changed again, sounding now like the snarl of a predatory animal.

"Never. If you're going to beat me or shoot me, you better do it now, because I'm not giving you any money. I won't open the safe. There's nothing you can do to me that'll force me to. Giving money to you would be like giving it to the devil himself."

Warner slapped her again. Tears sprang to her eyes, and she staggered back, catching herself on the edge of the library table.

"Nothing I can do? How about if I take you out to the barn and make you watch while I use your Mex friend as a target? I can shoot him in lots of places that won't kill him quick. Then I'd go to the bunkhouse and shoot some rabbits. There isn't a gunman in that entire crew of losers who hired on with you. What kind of a man would work for a woman boss, anyway, taking her orders and saying 'Yes, ma'am' a thousand times a day?" He spat on the floor at Lee's feet. "A coward, that's what kind—and that's all you've got here. Now, open the safe or I'll go ahead with what I just told you."

Lee locked her eyes with Warner's. *Would he really kill Carlos and the men?*

Suddenly, Warner's gun was in his hand. A shot like that of a cannon blasted through the room. The silver cross that hung on the wall spun to the floor, its right arm twisted upward where the bullet had struck it. The next shot kissed Lee's hair as it buzzed past.

"You looking to die?" Warner bellowed. He drew a deep breath. His face remained scarlet, but his voice was level. "Open the safe and save a few lives. I have nothing to lose by shooting you and your whole crew."

"It was all an act," Lee said. "Everything."

"Best stage play you ever saw, wasn't it? I had you, the law, the whole congregation, the whole town convinced I was a preacher. That's not easy to do for a man with a dozen notches on his pistol grips. I guess I owe it all to my parents." He laughed. "They sent me off to a theological school when I was twelve. I learned a lot there, before I got out when I was sixteen. I even acted in some plays, learned to control my voice, to speak properly, to handle myself in any situation. I killed my first man when I was seventeen. Outdrew the drunken old fool with a brand-new Smith & Wesson .38 I'd bought that very day."

He looked at the weapon he now held—a Colt .45— turning it from side to side in his hand. "I bought this one a couple years later. I needed more stopping power than the .38 could give me, so I went to a .45. It's never let me down yet."

Lee's eyes swept the office, searching for anything she could use as a weapon. The image of her Winchester 30.06 leaning against the wall next to her front door flashed in her mind. She'd put it there shortly after her house was built. But the Winchester was a room away— and it might just as well have been a mile.

"We can fix this," Lee said, her voice far less convincing than she wanted it to be. "Give me Missy's note and ride on. I'll see that the marshall doesn't come after you. You can get away clean."

Warner laughed. "Can you fix old lady Joplin being dead too?"

Lee stumbled back a step, feeling as if the floor had suddenly tilted. "You didn't . . ." she gasped.

"I probably did. I had to give her a pretty fair whack. It could have killed her. She sure wasn't moving when I pulled out."

Lee found the wall with her back and slid to the floor, her legs extended in front of her, dazed, not wanting to believe what Warner had said. Tears started in her eyes and flowed down her face. She made no move to wipe them away.

Warner watched her cry. Finally, he spoke. "I don't have time for this. Open the safe, and I'll be out of here in five minutes. I'm not going to ask again."

Lee awkwardly pushed herself to her feet. "I don't know the combination. I keep it in the drawer of the table in the parlor. You can find it there," she said, her voice a hoarse whisper.

"And leave you here all alone, correct?" He laughed. "One thing I'm not is stupid. Take the lantern and walk ahead of me. We'll go to the parlor together. Go on— move!"

Lee exaggerated her clumsiness as she reached for the wire handle of the lantern. "I'm dizzy," she murmured. "I'm afraid I'm going to faint."

Warner shoved her, starting her out the doorway. She moved her feet woodenly, almost shuffling, her mind spinning like a windmill blade in a hurricane. Again, she focused on her rifle. She swallowed hard when she realized that she'd have to click off the safety and work the lever to bring a bullet into the firing chamber. That would take perhaps a second—more time than she had. She weaved toward the table in front of the window. It was dark outside, and the yard in front of her house was empty and still. Nearby, a horse snorted wetly, extending the burst of air he blew through his nostrils. Lee stopped at the table and stood there facing it, holding the lantern, judging the distance to the window.

"Don't just stand there! Get the combination. Move!"

Lee sagged forward, shoulders drooping, and put her left hand out to steady herself on the table. Warner moved forward to hold her upright.

"Don't start any of this fainting stuff. I'm getting real—"

Lee bent at the waist, moaned, and then swung the lantern in an arc, slamming it into Warner's chest. Fuel slopped from it onto his shirt and immediately ignited from the flame at the top of the light. Warner yelled, dropped his gun, and beat at his chest with both hands, his scream becoming a rant of curses. Lee, free for the

187

moment, hurled the lantern through the window, smashing it and sending shards of glass flying to her front yard. She raised her arms to cover her face and, already in motion, followed the lantern out the window.

She hit the ground hard, but she hit it partially tucked into the beginning of a roll. Her breath left her in a loud whoosh as she rolled forward off her shoulders. She scrambled to get her feet under her and launched herself to the side, toward the house and around the corner, out of sight and out of the range of Warner's pistol.

Warner was at the window. With his arm poking through the broken glass and his pistol swinging from side to side, he looked for Lee. A slug dug a hole in the window frame, an inch from his head. Slivers of glass and wood sprayed him, the razorlike bits carving bleeding lines across his features.

"Warner!" Ben shouted from the yard. "Drop that gun and come out here!" In a lower voice, he added, "Lee, get Carlos to watch the back of the house!"

Warner recognized the voice. "Come on in and get me, Flood!" He fired a shot and dropped below the windowsill.

The lantern had smashed when it struck the ground. The remaining fuel caught fire and burned in an oval puddle. Light glinted on metal, and Ben threw himself to the side, firing once. Warner's bullet dug a furrow in the ground where Ben had been a half second ago.

Warner dared another look out the window, fired a couple of rounds at nothing, and backed away, the back of his leg knocking over Lee's rifle near the door. He holstered his pistol, grabbed the Winchester from the floor, and was jacking the lever when the door burst inward as if it had been struck by a battering ram.

The door missed him by few inches and crashed into the wall. The power of the impact threw the door back, and its edge bashed into Ben's side like a swing of an axe. The crack of a rib breaking was louder than the harsh breathing of the two men. Ben, wrenched to the side by the door, grasped clumsily at Warner and then struck the floor, his intended flying tackle now an awkward sprawl.

Warner snapped a shot at Ben's head with the rifle, missed, and banged the lever of the 30.06 downward, jamming the mechanism in his fury. He struggled with the lever for a moment, cursed, and swung the weapon by the barrel. The heavy, solid-wood stock caught Ben just above his ear.

Warner swung again and grazed Ben's head. So violent and enraged was his swing that the stock cracked and splintered, sending a numbing jolt of pain through both his arms. He flung the rifle aside and stood, drawing air and cursing. He reached for his Colt, but his fingers refused to obey. They fumbled about, touching the grips without grasping, fluttering from the sudden surge of disabling pain. His curses became a scream as he moved back a step and kicked Ben in the stomach and then the head.

Ben didn't move after Warner delivered the two blows with his boot. Blood puddled under and around his head, and the now-dying lantern-fuel fire made it glisten like ice on the polished hardwood floor.

He was drifting now, moving in currents of soft air that carried him as gently as a bit of plant fluff in a summer breeze. At the same time, someone—something—was tugging urgently at his left side. There was a hissing in his ears that grew louder, diminishing the pleasure

189

of floating. It was like the angry sound of a white-hot horseshoe plunging into water. And it didn't seem like an outside sound, but one that was coming from his own core—and it was becoming strident and shrill. The pressure on his left side was escalating too. It no longer pulled at him, but instead was pushing, crushing him, sending sharp tendrils of pain that made his ride on air a jagged, jerky sensation that was not at all a respite . . .

Ben's eyes popped open. Pain delivered a searing streak of torment to his left side, and his head rang with clamor and heat. He forced himself to a sitting position. His eyes took some time to focus, and when they did, they fixed on the shattered stock of Lee's Winchester. He pushed to his knees and then groaned his way to his feet, leaning against the wall.

There were voices outside the open door, but the words barely penetrated the screeching in Ben's head.

"Marshall? Marshall?" Two of Lee's ranch hands stood outside, neither one carrying a long gun or pistol. Ben stepped away from the wall and waved them back. At that moment, there was a crash from Lee's office loud enough to penetrate the noise in Ben's head. He lurched down the short hall, his fingers moving toward his pistol.

Warner stepped just outside the doorway to the office, a dark form in an even darker hall.

"You don't die easy, Flood."

"No easier than I have to. Get your hands up an' turn your back to me an' you might walk out of here." His words issued from a parched throat; they sounded weak.

Warner squared himself, moving his left boot back a few inches. "I'll tell you what, Flood: Drop your gun belt, and I'll let you live. You're in no shape to draw against me—and on the best day you ever had you couldn't beat me."

Ben shifted his shoulders slightly, and a bolt of pain screamed at him from his left side. Warner was no more than six feet away. He could smell the man's breath and sweat. He knew that Warner could right now be sliding his pistol from his holster.

Lee stormed through the back door, slamming it open so hard that it crashed against the wall. The lantern she carried shoulder high cast its harsh light into the hallway like a lightning bolt. "Ben!" she yelled. "Ben, are you all right?"

Warner's hand darted to his pistol. Ben's hand seemed to move on its own, drawing his Colt smoothly with no wasted motion, as quick as lightning striking a tree. At the same time, a wave of pain caused him to cry out. His right hand, its skills honed over the years, its muscles and tendons trained to never vacillate from their mission, raised the pistol and pulled the trigger twice.

Warner was punched back into the wall by the first slug. The next, the briefest part of a second later, caught him as he was falling. He hit the floor face first, his head almost touching Ben's right boot.

Ben saw Lee standing in the doorway, holding the lamp at shoulder height like a garden statue. Her eyes were fixed on him as he too slid to the floor. He didn't see her rush to his side.

The walk up the gentle slope took longer than it usually did for Ben and Lee. The moon was a brilliant white and hanging a few feet above the stillness of the prairie, and the air was mild; there was no breeze, and the boulders at Lee's special spot still held the warmth of the sun.

"Maria said Carlos is like a caged bear," Lee said. "She said he's the worst, most demanding patient in the world."

191

Ben smiled. "Carlos's head is too thick for anyone to really hurt."

"That's funny—he said the same thing about you."

Ben laughed and then wished he hadn't. Even with the tightly wrapped gauze holding his two fractured ribs in place, quick moves caused jolts of excruciating pain.

For a moment they sat in silence on the flat surface of a boulder they'd come to refer to as "the bench." Lee breathed in deeply, then spoke quietly. "It seems impossible that all that happened was only ten days ago. I'm so sorry. I hope you know just how sorry I am."

"We've been all through that, Lee. We were tricked, along with the church and the whole town. But it's over now. Warner's dead."

"Missy keeps calling him a whitened sepulcher."

"Well, that's what he was." Ben shifted his position and eased his right arm over Lee's shoulders. She sighed and snuggled against him more closely.

He cleared his throat. "I need to change some things in my life. I know that. I just need a little time."

"I need to make some changes too. We both need a little time."

"But together, right?"

"Yes, Ben—together."